ALL THE LIGHTS

ALL THE LIGHTS

Clemens Meyer

Translated by Katy Derbyshire

Introduced by Stuart Evers

First published in English in 2011 by
And Other Stories, 91 Tadros Court, High Wycombe, Bucks, HP13 7GF

www.andotherstories.org

Originally published as *Die Nacht, die Lichter*
© S. Fischer Verlag GmbH, Frankfurt am Main, 2008
English language translation copyright © Katy Derbyshire, 2011
Introduction © Stuart Evers

ISBN No. 978-1-908276-01-8

A catalogue record for this book is available from the British Library.

Supported by the National Lottery through Arts Council England.
The translation of this work was supported by a grant from the
Goethe-Institut which is funded by the German Ministry of Foreign
Affairs.

LOTTERY FUNDED

GOETHE
INSTITUT

CONTENTS

Introduction   vii

Little Death   3

Waiting for South America   13

The Shotgun, the Street Lamp and Mary Monroe   35

Fatty Loves   47

Of Dogs and Horses   59

I'm Still Here!   83

All the Lights   99

Riding the Rails   109

The Short Happy life of Johannes Vetterman   131

A Trip to the River   151

In the Aisles   167

A Ship Will Come   191

Your Hair Is Beautiful   201

Carriage 29   215

The Old Man Buries His Beasts   229

INTRODUCTION

The Terrifying Possibility of Now

The short story requires precision and economy; no matter how verbose the prose stylist, all writers are bound by its formal constraints. Even with this in mind, Clemens Meyer's work remains exceptionally lean, pared down, stripped bare. His stories are taut affairs, built – in the main – on short sentences, adjectiveless nouns and vernacular language. But while *All the Lights* appears simple, plain even, it swells and burns with complexity, subtlety and a strange kind of beauty. This is writing that basks in the terrifying possibility of now; that neither celebrates nor glamorises its cast of lost, lonely or otherwise impoverished characters, but presents them in situations that feel both authentic and devastatingly real. These are razor-blade slices of life, shorn of an overarching moral or social message.

The 'now' that each of the stories deals with is haunted by the past; it crops up in the most awkward places, stalks characters as they try to deal with the life the past has given them. In the opening story, 'Little Death', Meyer shows this confusion explicitly, hopscotching through time, allowing the past and the present to coexist in an uneasy, first-person present. Christian – if that is his name, we are never quite sure – is a construct of his own memory, a composite of all the people he has been and the person he has become, and the reader is left to piece his narrative together, from the loss of his silver wrist-watch, to leaving his apartment to sign on, to looking at the same apartment, evicted and drunk, passing a bottle to another victim of circumstance.

This blurring of time is at once confusing and dazzling: dreamlike shifts come together to form a unique depiction of lives unravelling and unspooling. While some stories are more conventional in approach – 'The Shotgun, the Street Lamp and Mary Monroe' is a junkie story with a twist; 'Fatty Loves' an exploration of misplaced love – Meyer always places considerable demands on his readers. He is not afraid to defy readerly expectation and refuses to take the easy road through his fictions.

In 'I'm Still Here!', a boxer is forced to defend himself from neo-Nazis and a pair of fight fans demanding compensation for the pugilist he's just put in hospital. We expect confrontation, violence, a set piece during which we can root for the gentle giant; instead most of the action takes place off-page, Meyer refusing to show the brawl or the tricks of his character's trade. The focus remains on the boxer's interior life, his small dreams of opening his own boxing club, of becoming more than his statistics. Just like life, none of Meyer's stories follow the trajectory you expect.

The lives Meyer depicts are small ones; ones lived in the margins of society. Their dreams are humble: finding enough money to buy drinks and cigarettes, to see the family one more time, to believe that things are better elsewhere. In 'Waiting for South America', perhaps the stand-out story in the collection, Frank receives letters from an old schoolfriend who claims to have made it big. For every description of a glorious Havana sunset or sip of thirty-year old rum, there is the humdrum of Frank's life to balance it: his money troubles, his ageing and infirm mother. Over the story's course, Meyer cleverly subverts the relationship between writer and receiver, asking questions that Frank is unwilling to pose, let alone answer. Nothing is certain, except, perhaps, the landscapes around them.

The topography of *All the Lights* is as constrained as Meyer's language: tenements, one-room apartments, corridors, bars, railway sidings, small-town shops. Water, whether rivers on which to skim stones or the sea inspiring dreams of escape, proves the only kind of redress to the oppressive urban tableau. And it's clear that Meyer understands this environment, its people and how its tone shifts from day into night. The sparse utility of his prose illuminates a drab former East Germany, pushing its characters into the light.

For all of Meyer's evident technical ability, it is his gift for character that sets him apart from writers ploughing similar furrows. The tender friendship between Blondie and the narrator of 'Riding the Rails' is based on larceny and deception, and a dwindling kind of communication. They don't need to finish sentences, don't need to explain their thoughts and feelings; the bond between them makes speech redundant. It takes remarkable confidence in a pair of characters to show them in such a light – they could so easily feel underwritten – but through this awkwardness the reader comes to understand them both, their dependence and their fears.

In an early interview, Clemens Meyer expressed his 'suspicion' of trying to define a generation, of any talk of a 'we' – 'everyone dies alone,' he added – and any attempt to bracket his writing as emblematic of post-reunification Germany is ultimately futile. What he has harnessed is a style that suits his concerns – part American minimalism, part post-modern European – and that he has fashioned it into his own. His is a voice that demands attention, unafraid to do different, sometimes seemingly wrong-headed, things, confident in its ability to move, confront and engage his readers.

Stuart Evers
June 2011

ALL THE LIGHTS

LITTLE DEATH

'See you around,' she says, picking up her bag from the bed. I nod and she leaves.

I hear her in the hallway. I haven't got a light out there and it takes her a while to find the door. I turn to face the wall, but she closes the front door very carefully. The leaving, the goodbye, the hand slipping down a shoulder and an arm into thin air, the lying still. And the dreams. The little death. No, death comes later, when you're alone and nobody comes any more.

I hear a train crossing the bridge. I turn my head and see the lights of the double-decker carriages through the blind. The train moves slowly; I can still hear it long after the lights have disappeared. I reach behind me for the table, looking for the cigarette I always put there, every time. I stopped smoking a while back now, it's just this one cigarette every time. I always go up to the guy with no teeth who lives right at the top, beforehand, a scrawny little man who lives with a fat woman.

'The cigarette,' he mumbles, grinning. He always calls me 'Christian', even though that's not my name, and I gaze at the last brown stumps left in his mouth. I always stay at the door, and he turns around, walks down the hall to the bedroom. I hear him rummaging around in there, and then the fat woman looks around the bedroom door. She's wearing some kind of nightshirt, her breasts resting on her stomach. She smiles, and I'm scared she'll come out. But the guy with no teeth shouts something, and she disappears. The place smells pretty strongly of spirits, and the guy with no teeth stinks like a meths-drinker once he's standing at the door again, clutching the cigarette in his scrawny hands. I hardly understand him when he talks, and it's not because almost all his teeth are gone. Sometimes I imagine the fat woman chewing his food for him. I take the cigarette and light it up. I turn onto my back and feel for the pillow, but I can't find it.

'You're so cold,' she says to me sometimes. I gaze at the ceiling. She's pulled the pillow over to her and she's lying a good way away from me with the pillow. I stretch my arm out towards her, but I only touch the pillow. I get up. I walk over to the window and look out through the blind over to the railway embankment. Stairs lead up to the station, lights glowing yellow. Here comes a man, walking down the stairs very slowly, and I turn away. 'You're so cold,' she says, and I feel my face with both hands, but it's warm.

'Are you going to the dole office tomorrow?' she asks. I nod. 'You didn't last week.'

'No. But I will tomorrow.' I flick the ash onto the

windowsill and lie back down next to the pillow. There's ash on the bedside table, and I blow it away. I've smoked the cigarette down to the filter and I balance the filter very carefully on the bedside table with the tip upwards. I watch the smoke rising, very straight, in a thin line. The glow at the tip slowly disappears and I close my eyes. I hear a train crossing the bridge, they come every twenty minutes until ten, I'll go and sign on, and if I get there early in the morning and it's quick and I can leave again quickly, then I can use the same ticket on the way back, but that's only happened two or three times over the years.

I walk down the bright white corridors, I'm tired and I see the numbers next to the doors, I fell asleep on the train, and the short man with the moustache woke me up, 'Appointments,' he says, 'appointments', he lives a couple of doors down but I didn't see him getting on. He signs on a lot, and I often see him on the train at other times, on his own by the window, maybe he sometimes rides from one end of the line to the other.

I walk down the bright white corridors, the short man's disappeared somewhere, I see the numbers next to the doors, chairs, people, and I sit down. Doors open, people disappear, people come out again and walk down the corridors, I look at the numbers next to the doors again, something's not right, and I get up. 'But this used to be . . .'

'No,' says the woman with the tag on her chest, I'm tired and I don't want to look at her chest, 'they're over in House B now.'

'House B,' I say and look around, but she's not here

any more. I push my sleeve back, but I haven't got a watch, where's my good silver watch? It was a present, but that was a few years back now. 'Appointments,' she says, 'so you always remember your appointments.'

I walk down the bright white corridors, the short man with the moustache is back again, standing in an open doorway, his back slightly bent.

He must be saying something, his head's moving, but all I hear is a woman's voice: 'And you've only come now?'

I walk past him to the lift. I press both buttons, one arrow pointing downwards, one pointing upwards, and I wait. There's a *ding*, but it's somewhere else, and I wait, and the lift comes very quietly, the doors open, and I walk in. No one else in there, and no mirror either. I press 'Ground Floor', the doors close, and we're on our way.

We're on our way. I look at my good silver watch. She holds onto my arm and says: 'We'll be late, you'll be late, they won't give you it because you're too late.'

I want to say something, but all I do is look at the hands on my watch. We're sitting on the train, she's holding onto my arm so tightly it hurts, and I look around for the short man with the moustache. 'Because you haven't got a car,' she says, and I try to push the sleeve of my jacket over my watch and her hand. I close my eyes and hear the train crossing the bridge. I open my eyes and see four cigarette filters balanced on the bedside table next to me. There's a *ding* and then a *dong*, and I get up. I walk over to the window and look outside through the blind. There's a man standing outside the door, behind him a small silver VW. Another *ding* and then *dong*, I want to go to the bell and disconnect it, I've been meaning to do that for a while now, but I walk over to the bed and lie down.

The bell goes quiet. He'll try somewhere else in a minute, but the building's empty, only the two beauties live at the very top, and I hope they're not in or that the fat woman's lying on top of him and he can't get to the buzzer, and that by the time she makes it to the door the little silver VW's disappeared.

I pull the cover up to my face, only my eyes are still there, and then, after a while – or was it just a few seconds? – I hear a car door slamming, and then another pause, engine noises. Then it's quiet. It's so quiet I'm scared the telephone might start ringing. I listen and wait. I don't want to pull the plug out, and maybe the line's been dead for ages already. They don't have to come round to cut you off.

'The cigarette,' mumbles the scrawny guy with a grin, and then he asks, 'Want to come in for a beer?' but I say, 'No, she'll be here soon,' and he grins at me, and it seems as if he has fewer teeth every time.

'Christian,' he mumbles with a wink. Once I did go in his flat, must have been a couple of years ago now because I still had a car back then, a silver VW Golf, something's not right, I had a little Japanese make and it was white. We watch TV, the scrawny guy drifts off to sleep, a bottle of spirits between his legs. I want to wake him up, but she holds onto my arm and takes the bottle. 'You're on your own a lot, Christian,' she says. 'No, no,' I say, 'she'll be here soon . . .'

'Christian,' she says, holding my hand now. Why don't

they know my name? I took the name sign off my door, but that was only a couple of weeks ago, and they've been living here for years, just like me. 'You're so cold,' she says.

We're on our way. Autumn's coming, and the last time we went to the lake was at the beginning of August, or was that the summer before? 'It's too cold to swim,' she says, but I say: 'We can just look at the water.' And I look. I've leant my bike against the tree and I look out at the lake. No one else here. It's a pretty small lake. The water's dark, that's because of the sky. There are a few letters in my jacket pocket, from the dole office, from the electricity board and from people I don't know. There's one from her too, and I walk up to the water so it's almost touching my shoes. A little wave comes now, there's a bit of a wind, but I stay where I am and throw the letters in the lake. They stay close to the bank for a while, then they spread out. I turn away and walk back to the tree. Behind the tree is a little embankment and after that the motorway. I can hear its humming. We're on our way. Along the embankment are little piles of rubbish, empty bottles, cigarette packs, paper. I ride slowly, turning around and looking at the water, but the letters have disappeared. When I turn around again I see one, a tiny speck of white by the bank. I ride and I don't look back again, because I know the little speck of white has disappeared.

I'm sitting on a bench by a country road. A few hundred yards ahead of me is a village, after that another one and then the city. Evening's coming, and the sky's red behind my back. I'm smoking a cigarette, I don't know where I got it from, it's not the brand the scrawny guy smokes. I haven't been to see him in a long time, sometimes I just hear his beauty, that's what he calls her, dragging the empty dustbins through the building and out into the yard when the bin men have been. Maybe the cigarette's from the short man with the moustache, but he rolls his own. 'Got into the habit when I was doing service,' he says. 'Where did you do your service?' I ask. 'Here and there,' he says, 'I did plenty of it,' and I know what he means. He has a couple of tattoos and a couple of kids, who play up on the railway embankment almost all day long. 'Because I was away so long,' says the short man and raises his shoulders so high that his head almost disappears, 'I did plenty of service.' His wife is just as short as he is; I see her sometimes fetching the kids in from the embankment. There are two flies perched on my leg. They're not moving, not even when I try to blow them off. It's the time of year when the flies die. They're just perched on my leg, close together, now one of them moves its wings, just for a moment, and I get up carefully.

Ten o'clock. The blue zero turns into a one. It took me a long time to find an alarm clock with a blue digital display. We were in a shop where they only had clocks and watches. Did she buy me the good silver watch there? The little blue one turns into a two. I'm standing in the dark, not moving. It's not getting light this morning, that's because of the sky. The digital display on the alarm clock is empty, but I watch the hands on my wrist. The electricity board came round, and the flat's dark. I don't know how long now, and I miss the little blue numbers. I want to lie back down, but I can't make out the pillow. They rang up a lot; the phone works even in the dark. 'Why didn't you come to your appointment?' I want to tell them about the short man with the moustache, who doesn't take the train any more, but all I say is, 'I've been very tired recently.'

'We're going to have to cut your benefits.'

'It's because of my alarm clock,' I want to say, but they're sure to know about the good silver watch on my wrist.

'It's me,' she says somewhere, and I say, 'How's it going, where are you?'

'I'm fine,' she says, 'I rang your bell, a couple of times.'

'Must have been out for a walk,' I say, and then there's a click, somewhere out there where she is, and I know that sound. It's a lighter, and she doesn't smoke.

I hold the phone away from my head; the click's still moving in my ear. 'Where are you?' I say and hear her voice and then I stay quiet and wait for it to click again, a different sound, a very different sound, and she's gone. I walk over to the bedside table and pick up the lighter. I flick it on and off again and on again. I've arranged the filters in a circle. I let the flame burn for a bit, and then I want to hear the sound again. The little death. Not a sound in the flat, even the fridge is silent in the kitchen. I put the lighter carefully on the pillow and walk over to the window. I look out through the blind over to the railway embankment. The lights are glowing yellow; it must be evening already.

I stand in the yellow light and look at the street and then at my building. All the windows are dark, even the scrawny guy and his beauty are sitting in the dark; or maybe they've gone out, it's the beginning of the month. There's a bar down the road, but maybe they've gone to the Italian place a bit further away, the scrawny guy sucking spaghetti into his toothless mouth, and her watching him with a smile.

I sit down on the stairs, jamming the bottle between my legs. I screw off the top and throw it away. A couple of cars drive past, it's turned cool now, and I drink. Then the light goes on, right at the top on the fourth floor. The curtains are pulled back but there's no one to see at the window, just a big teddy bear sitting on the windowsill. I feel myself smiling. I hear the train behind me and the cars down on the road, but all I can see is the big teddy bear in the middle of the windowsill. I don't know how long I look at it, I feel the smile in the corners of my mouth, then I pick up the bottle and put my head back and drink. There's a plane in the sky, it leans slightly to one side and curves round to the airport outside the city.

'How's it going?'

I take the bottle from my lips and hand it to the short man. His moustache has gone, his face is swollen, his top lip hidden under a large plaster. He puts his head back and drinks and watches the plane.

Then he sits down next to me. 'They gave me magic stitches,' he says with a tap of his top lip. 'They dissolve after a while, all on their own.' He tries to smile but stops again; it must hurt. 'Magic stitches,' I say, and he nods. He hands me one of his roll-ups. 'Do you still take the train?' I shake my head, and he nods again. He's sitting pretty close to me, and I feel him going all limp and leaning his shoulder against me. We drink, in silence.

I'm standing at the window, looking out through the blind over at the railway embankment. The lights are glowing yellow; it must be evening already. There's a man standing in the yellow light. He turns away.

WAITING FOR SOUTH AMERICA

His mother was sitting in the dark. 'What's the matter?' he said. 'Aren't you going to turn the light on? It's getting late.'

'Oh no,' she said, 'I like sitting here watching it get dark.' She was in her seat, right by the window, and the last light of dusk fell on her hands and the table. He saw the candles, and now he knew she wasn't watching it get dark out of choice. They'd cut off her electricity. He looked at the date on his watch: the twentieth, more than ten days to go until she'd get her money. And he had to wait more than ten days as well; he was used to waiting, after all the years he'd been waiting now. 'I'll be off then, mother,' he said.

'Yes,' she said, 'I've got things to do as well.'

'Shall I leave you something here? I'm flush right now.' He knew she'd say no. It was only once he was outside in the stairwell that he remembered his eye, thought it was maybe quite a good thing his mother was sitting in the dark, so she couldn't see it. It wasn't that bad, not even very swollen, just a small dark blue, almost black crescent under his eye that wouldn't go away, for days now, even though he pressed ice cubes on it and used some gel from the chemist's. He didn't even remember exactly how it had happened any more, some young lad in some local bar. He hadn't started it himself, he was quite sure about that – when he was at a bar drinking away his money, even though there were over fourteen days to go, all he wanted was to be left in peace and to forget everything. Maybe he hadn't been watching out and had barged against someone, and some of these young lads were damn quick to pack a punch and start fights over nothing. Most of them were waiting just like he was, just not for as long. But they were waiting all right, for work, for money.

He walked the streets, not looking left or right; he knew everything here, every street, every building, he'd been living round here for over forty years, and he heard the voices from the open windows, the clatter of plates, children, and he felt the people walking past him, and he saw the yellow light of the street lamps and the brightly coloured lights of the bars and shops out of the corner of his eye. Only a couple of bars had kept going, there'd been one on every other corner in the old days, and the little shops had started disappearing as well.

He walked past the playground where the young people met up in the evenings and at night, and he could hear them now as well, maybe the lad who'd given him the black eye was even there.

Someone said, 'Excuse me, sir,' and he took a step to one side and asked, 'How are you?' And the woman with the big twin buggy who lived a couple of doors down from him smiled and said, 'Oh, not bad.' She tapped a finger to her eye and then asked, 'I hope that was nothing serious,' but she had dark circles under her own eyes, sometimes so dark that when he met her in the street it looked like she'd taken a couple of punches too. 'No, no,' he said. 'Just been doing a bit of sport.' She nodded and pushed the buggy past him, and he eyed her baggy jeans that looked two sizes too big.

He stood in front of his letterbox. He hadn't checked it for post for a few days now, and as he turned the tiny key in the lock and opened the door of the box, three letters fell to the floor at his feet. He bent down and picked them up. One from the job centre and one from a company he'd applied to ages ago, and he knew there was no point reading it but tore open the envelope anyway. He pulled out the folded sheet of paper, held it into the light of the stairway lamp, then he screwed it up and put it in his pocket with the empty envelope and the letter from the job centre. He held the third letter in his hands for a while until the light went out automatically. He stood in the dark, stroking the envelope. He could feel the stamp. There was a large butterfly on it, so brightly coloured that he thought he could still make it out in the dark, and above the butterfly were the large capital letters 'CUBA'. He didn't know anyone in Cuba. He had turned the letter over, but there was no sender on the back, no name, no address. He switched the light on and went up the stairs slowly with the letter. He lived right at the top on the fourth floor, and as he climbed up one step at a time he kept thinking over and over, 'Cuba, Havana, Cuba'. Maybe the letter was for someone else, but his address and his name were written large and clearly on the envelope. He unlocked his front door, put the key in the lock from inside and turned it twice, and then he turned on the light. He thought about his mother and about how he'd have to pay again soon or they'd come round to his place too. Cuba. He hung his jacket on the peg, went into the kitchen and put the letter down on the table, right in the light of the lamp. Then he took a beer out of the fridge but put it back again and made coffee. He had hardly any money left, and the beer had to last another ten days. He could take back deposit bottles, he had over forty empty beer bottles on his small balcony, plus a few mineral water and cola bottles; he'd get a couple more beers for the deposit money but he was ashamed of turning up with large, clinking bags full at the supermarket with the local drinkers standing around outside. The only times they weren't there were when it was particularly cold in winter. Why don't I take a small bag to the supermarket, he thought, and get rid of the bottles bit by bit? He poured himself a cup of coffee, milk and sugar, then he sat down at the table. He drank a sip, a few drops of coffee spilt on the table, and he fetched a cloth and wiped across the tabletop a few times, then put the cup down on the cloth. He sat down again. He examined the letter, trying to recognise the handwriting, but he hadn't got any private post for ages now, only from the benefits office and companies he'd applied to. He held the letter up to the light but he couldn't make anything out in the envelope. The postmark had 'Cuba' in it too, and then there were a few little numbers, probably the date, he could read '08' but the rest was smudged; perhaps it had got wet on its travels. Had the letter come by ship or on a plane? But then it would say 'Air Mail' on the postmark, wouldn't it? His mother had got a letter from New York once, from a cousin, and he'd read something about 'Air Mail' on the envelope. 'Paula's on holiday in New York, imagine that, New York, an eight-hour flight, you do remember your second cousin Paula, don't you?' But he couldn't remember a Paula, and what did he care about planes and ships and New York?

He tore the letter open, he tore it open so roughly that he broke the butterfly, and then he was holding a sheet of A4 paper in his hand, densely covered in writing. The writing was so small that he got up again to fetch his reading glasses from the front room. He had to look for them for a while; they were on the windowsill. He put them on and peered over the lenses out of the window. It was night now, and he saw the dark houses opposite, lights only burning in a couple of windows. There were lots of empty places round here. He tugged the curtains closed and went back into the kitchen. He sat down and drank a mouthful of coffee. The coffee was just right now, not too hot any more, and he drank another mouthful.

He gave a loud cough before he started reading.

Dear Frank,

It's been a while since we heard from each other, and it's been even longer since we've seen each other. Three or four years? I can't remember exactly. Before you start puzzling or look all the way to the bottom,

where I've written 'With best wishes, Wolfgang', I
can't help laughing now because I've only just started
writing.

He put one finger on the line he was reading and smoothed
the paper with the other hand. Wolfgang. He only knew one
Wolfgang, his old schoolfriend Wolfgang, who he'd grown
up with round here. What on earth was Wolfgang doing in
Cuba? He'd been out of work, just like him, he'd been waiting, just like him. Two years ago or so Wolfgang had called
him from Berlin, said he had better chances of finding
work there.

You'll be wondering what I'm doing in Cuba. It's all
muddled up in my head, because I'm on my way to
South America. Brazil. Remember how we used to
dream of Brazil? Pelé, the great Pelé. The white Sugarloaf Mountain and the girls on the beach, remember
that? We were ten back then, the 1970 World Cup.
That was in Mexico. Brazil versus Italy in the final. We
watched it at my uncle's bar. And the semi-final too,
West Germany versus Italy. That was a great game,
4–3 for Italy, I remember it really clearly because
my uncle threw a bottle of spirits at the screen after
extra time. Rudi had a bet on that Germany would be
world champions. You do remember my Uncle Rudi,
don't you? That little bar down by the park. Is the
building still there? What's in there now? Uncle Rudi
sold his bar in summer '89 and went to the West. But

you probably know that yourself anyway.

So you still live in our part of town, that's good, someone has to keep the flag flying, even when times are hard.

Frank, I've got rich. No, don't worry, I haven't robbed a bank like I joked about once, years ago. I don't think I could have done it, just walked into a bank and pulled out some gun. Even if I'd been out of work to the end of my days, I'd have tried to get through it with decency.

Frank, I'm almost a bit embarrassed to write to you from Cuba that I've got rich. I heard things aren't going all that well for you, and you're still my oldest and best friend, even though we haven't seen each other for so long, and I hope my letter gives you strength and courage. One of the old guard has made it!

But you know I've always been a bit boastful, so I have to backtrack a bit. I haven't got really rich of course, but it's more money than I've ever had in my life. If I invest it well and spend it a bit carefully I'll probably be able to live off it a few years, but you know me, I've never been that good with money and I'll probably never learn to be, even though I'm trying not to spend it like water. But I want to see a little piece of the world and tell you about it. I'm forty-six now, like you, but I don't want to start on about how time passes, because you know that just as well as I do. I'm just drinking thirty-year-old rum, do you remember, thirty years ago, maybe a bit longer even, we got really drunk for the first time. We puked our guts out in Uncle Rudi's bar, but I still like thinking about that night, and I am right now, as I'm drinking this wonderful rum, it's really dark in the glass, almost black. I'm sitting on the balcony, in a small hotel right on the sea. A beach I've never seen the likes of, all white, and the sea's green and then further out it goes blue again. Turquoise – I'd only seen it in photos. And I want to write about the evening sun, which is so huge, but I can't help thinking of us sitting at Uncle Rudi's bar and drinking that cheap blended rum and imagining we were in Rio de Janeiro drinking the very finest rum with fresh mint in it, with the sea and Sugarloaf Mountain outside, and coffee-coloured Brazilian beauties dancing tango on the beach. Tango in Brazil. And we were happy somehow when we daydreamed like that, even though we usually puked really badly afterwards. Yesterday I was in a bar in Havana where they had over a hundred kinds of rum. Some of the bottles from before we were even born. And cigars, the very finest Cuban cigars, hand rolled, I'll try and send you one but I don't know if it'll get through customs. But to stop you wondering, I'll tell you how I came into the money. Uncle Rudi died. He didn't get much money for his bar back then. He really wanted to go to the West, and six months later the Wall came down but he never came back, and nobody knew what he was doing. He never wrote either, I didn't even know he was still alive. And then I get a letter, and

then I find out that my Uncle Rudi, the crazy old gee-
zer, had a thriving bar in Hamburg. Can you imagine
Uncle Rudi behind the counter of a good, posh bar?
I couldn't either, but that's just how it was. All those
years, Uncle Rudi had a smart little bar on the Kiez,
and he put money aside. You know my parents have
been dead for over ten years now, he was my mother's
brother, and Uncle Rudi never married and never had
children either. He never got in touch in all the years,
but I was in his will, just me. And I bet there would
have been much more money left if he hadn't had such
a grand lifestyle, but you know Uncle Rudi. It's nearly
dark now. If only I could describe this huge red sun
on the ocean. I have to get a camera, I didn't even
think of that, but it is my first big trip.

There's a little road down in front of the hotel,
where real vintage cars drive past sometimes. There
are hardly any new cars in Cuba because of the em-
bargo. I've never seen such amazing vintage models,
Chevrolets with big hood ornaments, ancient black
Fords, some of the cars are put together out of several parts of different makes, but they drive.

Frank, I wish I could shake your hand. Say hello to
everyone when you're walking round our part of town.
I'll write again soon, no matter where I travel next.

Your old friend, Wolfgang

He was on the balcony between the empty beer bottles.
They clinked quietly whenever he moved. He had folded up

the letter and was holding it in one hand. He looked at the dark houses, blue light flickering in a few windows now. He held a glass in the other hand, cheap Jamaican blended rum, he'd gone to the all-night garage specially and bought himself a small bottle, even though it cost almost three times as much as at the shops. In winter, he sometimes had rum in the house, because he liked to make himself a hot toddy when he was cold, but it wasn't even autumn yet. He took a swig. The stuff tasted terrible; he never drank it straight usually but that didn't matter right now. He raised his glass and moved it to and fro in front of his face, and the rum moved in the glass and looked almost black in the darkness. He had turned out the light in the kitchen, the balcony door was pushed to, and he heard the quiet hum of the fridge. He was still holding the letter tightly in his left hand, he had taken it along to the garage, had held it so tightly all the way that he could see his fingerprints on it as he stood in front of the spirits section and put the letter in his jacket pocket and took the bottle off the shelf with his damp and trembling hand.

As he walked back home he held the letter in his left hand and the bottle of rum in his right like a small club. Grown men and teenage lads walked past him towards the garage, some with empty cloth or plastic bags, some looking at the ground, others looking him right in the eye and barging into him slightly, but he broadened his shoulders under his jacket, walked along the middle of the pavement and held the letter at chest level so that everyone could see it, as if they'd understand then that his old friend Wolfgang was sitting by the sea in Cuba, watching the big red evening sun and drinking rum with all his money. '. . . and I hope my letter gives you strength and courage. One of the old guard has made it!'

He turned around and saw the neon lights of the garage, a good way away now, a sign shining blue on the roof. It blurred when he squinted, and he tried to imagine a roaring sound, louder and louder, just the roar and the blue. A couple of mopeds rattled along the road. He turned his head slightly and saw a girl sitting behind the driver, both arms raised and laughing.

The bottle was empty. Just a sip left in the glass. He leant against the balcony wall. The night had turned cold but he didn't feel it.

'I'm standing on top of an ancient Mayan pyramid on the Yucatán Peninsula in the south of Mexico. If you look at a map you'll see it's not far from Cuba to Yucatán.'

He took his old school atlas out of the cloth bag he'd brought specially. It was a very large atlas, and he had to rest it on both knees and wedge the letter under the atlas, and the people sitting next to him and against the opposite wall gave him slightly strange looks. He flicked through the pages, looking; he had opened the letterbox as he went to leave the house. He had sat down on a step and started reading. Then he'd run back upstairs again, he didn't want to miss his tram, had torn the old school atlas off the shelf, put it in a slightly stained cloth bag, slammed the front door without locking it and run down the stairs to the tram stop. He saw the tram coming round the corner in the distance, he ran and waved, the bag banging against his leg, and as he jumped on through the closing door the bag got trapped and he had to tug it out roughly, and then he sat down, breathing heavily. He wanted to get the atlas out and read more of the letter but the tram got more and more crowded at every stop.

He flicked through and looked, Canada, northern USA, the North West, Mexico, there right on the edge was Yucatán, but where was Cuba? He turned more pages, Central America and the Caribbean. Then he saw the Yucatán peninsula again, large and wide, and a little way above the tip was the narrow, long-drawn shape of Cuba. He put his forefinger on the map and then his thumb. The sea was only a thumb's width between Yucatán and Cuba. Did Wolfgang go over on a little boat? How long must he have been at sea? A fishing boat, a little fishing boat, bobbing on the very top of the waves and then vanishing and then popping up again. He pulled the letter out from under the atlas and laid it on Venezuela and the Antilles. 'Chichén Itzá is the largest Mayan city in Central America. From up here I can see the dense jungle, green without end. I've rented out a little hut nearby, and at night the jungle makes noises, whistling, singing, high-pitched screams like children, I reckon the birds and the other animals hardly ever sleep.'

'Mr Mose, please!' A woman's voice, and he saw the woman standing in the open doorway, calling out again, 'Mr Mose, please!' And her voice seemed high and shrill now, the birds and the other animals hardly ever sleep. Mr Mose walked past him, giving him a dirty look because he laughed and Mr Mose must have thought he was laughing at him like the kids used to laugh at his name. A door slammed, and then he carried on reading, one finger on the little black dot on the map next to the words 'Chichén Itzá'.

'I've been here ten days now, wandering around the old Mayan city and the jungle and the little town nearby with all its clay huts. There's a bar there, they call them *cantinas* here. Have you ever drunk tequila? Some people in the *cantina* drink it like water, even though it's hot and muggy here. They drink it with salt and lemon, first the salt on your tongue, then you knock back the tequila, then you bite into the lemon. I saw it once in a bar in Berlin, but I had to come to Mexico to try it out for myself. Go into some bar, Frank, and drink a tequila to my health, maybe I'll be sitting in the *cantina* at the same time, drinking to you. I saw something really beautiful a couple of days ago. A woman showed me it. She's beautiful as well, and she's not just any old woman. She's a Red Indian woman, an *India* as they say here, and when the jungle's so noisy at night she sits and lies with me. Frank, a Red Indian woman, imagine that! I can't help thinking of how we played Red Indians as kids, and there was that little girl from down our road who used to be our squaw. And Maria Pilar, who's something like my squaw now, looks just the way I always used to imagine a Red Indian woman. Skin like bronze, and hair so black it shines like fresh shoe polish. And she smells really different, she has a special smell, slightly sweet and bitter, not like the

women in Germany who stink of either perfume or sweat.'
Another name was called, somewhere at another door, and
again Frank looked up for a moment and saw a woman sitting next to him; she hadn't been sitting there before. He
leant over slightly in her direction and took a deep breath
through his nose. Then he thought of his wife, who'd been
a friend of the little girl they used to play Red Indians with
as kids. He thought of how long he hadn't seen her now, but
he didn't want to see her any more, he was glad she was a
long way off, just sad that she'd taken Klara with her and
he could only see her once or twice a year. He ran a hand
through his hair a couple of times; it was still quite thick,
only thinning a tiny bit at the temples. Hadn't Wolfgang
been almost bald? Bald Wolf with his young squaw.

'I like her a lot, but you know I want to keep going to
Brazil. Not right now or tomorrow, but one day, maybe soon,
I can feel it. But I wanted to tell you what the beautiful
thing was that she showed me. She came to my hut in the
evening and took me by the hand and led me to a little
hill. The sun was very low in the sky, and it was almost
dark, and the light and the shadows of the setting sun fell on
the steps of the Kukulcán Pyramid and made the shape of a
giant snake winding down the steps.

'There's nothing to see there usually, only the stone
steps, but now this giant snake seemed to be creeping towards us. Then I saw all the tourists standing around the
pyramid, but we were all alone on our hill. Maria Pilar only
speaks a tiny bit of English and I only have a few words of
Spanish, but later someone told me it happens exactly twice

every year, every twenty-first of March and twenty-third of September. And as I was standing there on the little hill with Maria Pilar . . .' He closed the atlas shut. He looked at the date on his watch, even though he knew very well it was the twenty-eighth of September today. How did the letter get to him from the jungle in such a short time? 'Mr Eisner, room thirty-two please!' He put the atlas with the letter in it in his bag. Maybe there was a little airfield there somewhere. Wolfgang had money . . . Or he'd been standing up at the top of the pyramid, the night was very bright, and he wrote the letter up there. Weren't the nights always very bright in the tropics? Five days to Germany, of course, why not? Maybe Wolfgang had gone up again on his own the next morning. Maria Pilar was waiting for him in his hut, she'd made strong Mexican coffee. He gazed at the vast jungle, green all the way to the horizon, thought of home and his old friend and took out pen and paper. 'Mr Eisner, room thirty-two please!' He said, 'Yes,' took his bag and saw the letter between the pages of the atlas and stood up.

He had got three letters now and he'd been waiting for the fourth one for months. In his last letter, Wolfgang had written about leaving Mexico, about leaving Maria Pilar, the beautiful Red Indian woman. 'Do you know what I called her? *Mi clara estrella*, that means "my bright star". And the stars up above us at night were really so bright, not like anything I've ever seen in Germany. They seemed to be incredibly close too, right above the trees. She's all alone in Chichén Itzá now but I promised to go back to her, maybe then I'll take her with me to Brazil. You know I've always been a dreamer, but I swear on our friendship that I'll marry that wonderful woman one day, but first I have to travel. South America, you know.' The letter was from Honduras, from the capital city Tegucigalpa, there was an airport there, and Wolfgang wanted to fly to Brazil from there.

He was in the bar that had once belonged to Wolfgang's Uncle Rudi. Everything had been stripped down and converted; he hadn't even recognised the building. Back then it had been a real German corner bar with wooden tables and wood-panelled walls. Now it was one of those modern places, neon lights and brightly coloured cocktails served by young girls.

He'd been to see his mother; he'd saved a bit of money and put it secretly in her little savings box. He'd taken a twenty-euro note out again, and now he was sitting at the black bar, which was made of cool metal, and drinking. He was drinking tequila like Wolfgang had suggested. He'd been here a couple of times now and drunk tequila. He moistened the little dip between his thumb and forefinger with his tongue, then sprinkled a little salt on the wet spot, took the glass in one hand and the slice of lemon in the other, licked the salt from his hand, knocked back the alcohol and then bit into the slice of lemon until tears pricked his eyes. 'To you,' he said, 'to you and Maria Pilar and Brazil.'

The year was almost over, the nights were getting frosty but there was no snow. It was summer in Brazil right now, and soon Wolfgang would be celebrating New Year in summer, if he was in Brazil by now. 'Another tequila please,' he said, 'and a beer.' The young woman behind the bar nodded. It was nearly ten and he wanted to go home soon. He had to get up early; he had a place on a job creation scheme now, working at a tourist information stall in town. An old man sat down on one of the bar stools next to him, knocked on the bar and nodded at him. Frank knocked back at him and smiled. The old greeting in a bar. The barmaid put the beer and the tequila down in front of him. 'I'll have a large one as well,' said the old man. The young woman took a glass and went to the pump. The old man turned around to him. 'They drink cocktails here now,' he said, 'but back in the old days . . .' He leant on the counter and looked Frank right in the face.

'You live round here, don't you?'

'Yes,' he said. 'Always have done.'

'I'm from round this way myself.' The old man pulled a pack of cigarettes out of his pocket and put them down in front of him, searching through his pockets again and putting a lighter on top of his cigarettes. Frank looked at his thin, wrinkled fingers.

'Thanks,' said the old man, and took the beer from the barmaid's hand and drank. He tipped his head back, then he put the glass on the bar and wiped the foam from his chin. 'Oh, sorry,' he said. He raised his glass again, and Frank picked up his beer as well, and they clinked glasses. 'To the old beer-drinkers.' Frank took a drink and laughed and said, 'To us old beer-drinkers,' then he knocked back his tequila, without the salt and lemon.

'You know this place from the old days, do you?'

'You can say that again,' said the old man. 'It was pretty much my second home.' He took a cigarette out of the pack and lit it up. 'One for yourself?'

'No thanks. I never started smoking. Just a good cigar every now and then.'

'Oh aye,' said the old man, 'a good cigar's a good cigar. Can't hardly beat that.' He tipped his head back and blew the smoke up to the brightly coloured lamps on the ceiling.

'You used to come here quite often in the old days, am I right?'

'Yes,' said Frank, 'quite often. But that's about thirty years ago now.'

'Thirty years.' The old man breathed out loudly. He leant against the bar again, and again he looked him right in the face. 'You were a friend of Rudi's nephew, weren't you?'

Frank drank a swig of beer and nodded. He tried to remember – who could this old man be? He must have been about the same age then as Frank was now. Round about. But there'd been so many regulars at Rudi's, spending their evenings and their days at the bar or one of the round wooden tables.

'I knew it right away.' The old man pressed out his cigarette. 'I used to know them well, Rudi and his nephew. Often saw you two here. Rudi was risking his licence serving you two alcohol.'

'Yes,' said Frank. 'But we never went over the top.'

The old man gave him a wink. 'I remember differently.' He drank his glass dry and pushed it across the bar. The barmaid had turned the music up – something electronic with a lot of bass, and Frank heard voices behind him but didn't turn around. Then there were a couple of young lads next to him, ordering something, and he saw the barmaid juggling bottles and chopping up a couple of limes. 'I always got him the best stamps back then.'

'Stamps?' Frank emptied his glass and pushed it next to the old man's. 'Two more,' he said, 'and two tequilas,' and the barmaid said, 'Be with you in a minute.'

'I worked for the post office,' said the old man, 'in the old days.' And suddenly Frank knew who he was. They'd sat at Rudi's bar and turned the pages of the big stamp album. 'Two new Pelé stamps,' said Wolfgang. 'Really rare, no post-mark.' They looked at the stamp and the tiny Pelé, who seemed to be holding an even smaller ball on the tip of his foot, and the longer they gazed at Pelé, their heads resting on their hands, the quieter it got around them, the noise of the pub fell silent, and then the ball danced on the tip of Pelé's foot, and then Pelé too moved on the little stamp.

Frank took a deep breath. 'He made some money, Rudi did. Came into a lot of money, over in Hamburg.'

'Money?' The old man sniffed at the tequila. 'Is this *Korn*?' He was used to German spirits.

'No,' said Frank. 'Just do what I do.' He moistened the small dip between his thumb and forefinger with his tongue, sprinkled a little salt on the wet spot, handed the saltshaker to the old man and waited for him to do the same. 'And now the lemon.' The old man smiled, and they took the slice of lemon in one hand, the glass in the other, then they licked the salt from their hands, tipped back the alcohol and bit into the slice of lemon, 'Ahhh, Jesus, what's that?!' and then the old man laughed and asked, 'Rudi made money?'

He was running through the night. It was really cold, and his breath came steaming out of his mouth. He could still hear the old man laughing – 'Rudi made money, you're telling me Schnapps-Rudi made money out of a bar in Hamburg!' He couldn't understand why the old man was laughing so wildly. He slowed down now, putting his hands in his jacket pockets and passing the playground, which was dark and empty. Where did the young lads go when it was so cold? Maybe to some bar or other, if they had any money.

'And the stars up above us at night were really so bright, not like anything I've ever seen in Germany. They seemed to be incredibly close too . . .'

They were bright, the stars up above him, not a cloud in the sky, but they must have shone much brighter over there, and close . . . no, they seemed tiny and far away to him. He kept walking. He took out his key, even though he was still a good way away from home. He jangled the keys, the street was empty and silent, and he could hear his footsteps. 'You know I've always been a dreamer, but I swear . . . but first I have to travel.' He unlocked the door to his building. He stood in the dark stairwell and looked for the keyhole, then he locked the door again, once, twice. He turned on the light and stopped in front of the letterboxes on the wall. 'Everything's muddled in my head; I'm on my way to South America.'

Maybe Wolfgang hadn't written for so long because he'd taken Maria Pilar to Brazil. He was certain the two of them had long since seen Sugarloaf Mountain. The light went out automatically, and he switched it on again and jangled his keys as he walked up to his flat. He tried to jangle his keys so it sounded kind of South American. What did they dance in Brazil? Salsa, cha-cha-cha? He'd bought himself a book about Brazil; it had said something about samba schools, next to photos of beautiful women wearing next to nothing, decorated with sequins and feathers. He had sat at the kitchen table night after night looking at the photos, not just the ones of the beautiful women. The Church of São Francisco with all its gold, the white foaming waterfalls of Iguaçu, Guanabara Bay off Rio de Janeiro. He jangled his keys, stamping his feet as he walked, and then he started whistling, trying to whistle a tune that matched with the jangling and stamping. Once he reached his front door on the fourth floor he went silent and took a deep breath.

'I'm standing on the peak of Sugarloaf Mountain, looking down at Guanabara Bay. It's night, and there are lights everywhere on the little islands, and between the islands and further out are the lights of the ships. Behind me the sky is bright, no stars. Rio de Janeiro.'

THE SHOTGUN, THE STREET LAMP AND MARY MONROE

The room I'm sitting in is pretty small and shitty. There are shittier rooms, in jail and that.

No. I open my eyes. I'm not in my little room at all, my little one-room flat, I like my little one-room flat, but I kind of lost control of everything there. There's too much stuff on the floor, the shelves are empty; just a few plates on them with dried-on leftovers. And now that the weather's getting warmer the flies and other creepy-crawlies are having a ball, and it's all theirs now because I don't go to my little flat any more. But I took my shotgun with me. It's a great shotgun, an air rifle, .177 calibre. It's a spring-piston rifle; you have to pull back the cocking lever before every shot to produce the air pressure. The butt and the shaft of my shotgun are made of beautiful brown wood and the gun looks pretty real, like a carbine. But it's not as if I take my shotgun with me everywhere. It's actually a shotgun for at home. I used to spend hours shooting at the flies. Once I got a spider, one of those long, thin-legged spiders that don't live in webs. Got it right in the middle of its little body. I didn't hit first time – the wall and ceiling were covered in bullet holes, and when I did hit it its little body got stuck in the wall and the long thin legs kept moving for a while. That did my head in. I chucked the gun in the corner, and if I'd been religious I'd have said a prayer for that poor spider. But that's stupid really; I've never had a good relationship with spiders. I don't have a good relationship with a lot of people, but I've never actually shot one. I have to admit, I'm scared of a lot of people and all, just like I'm scared shitless of spiders. Like, there's a bar down on the ground floor of the building where my one-room flat is, the flat I've left to the flies and all the other creepy-crawlies. It's called 'Feasters' Retreat', and there are always hundreds of Neo-Nazis in there, feasting. Usually on beer and spirits. I've had a drink in there once or twice, and every time I wished I'd taken my shotgun down with me. But I bet they'd only have laughed at my beautiful spring-loader. You can do a lot of damage with the butt, though. And the thing has a twenty-shot magazine, and I wouldn't very much like to get one of those 0.177-inch balls of lead in the eye.

'Sweetheart,' I call out. 'Sweetheart,' and then I hide my shotgun under the sofa. She doesn't like my shotgun, that's why. I don't know if she can see me; the bedroom door's open. My sweetheart doesn't like my shotgun, so I only get it out when my sweetheart's in the bedroom. But she's not asleep. She's lain down in bed because she's angry with me.

Oh shit, what have I done now? 'Sweetheart,' I call out,

making my voice all gentle, the way she likes it. I'm a master at making my voice gentle the way women like it. But my sweetheart's the only one I want to love my gentle seduction voice. And I really love that girl, even when she's angry with me and hiding in the bedroom. And I think she loves me too, or she wouldn't have stuck it out with me so long in my one-room flat. She already had her flat back then, the one I'm in now, but the thing was I couldn't leave my flat, I used to hide out in bed, and she'd sit on the edge of the bed and wipe my forehead and really sweet things like that. She didn't even have a go at me for having my shotgun in bed next to me. The shotgun had to go though, whenever she slept next to me. But I was clever; I squeezed my little rifle in the wee gap between the wall and the bed so I could always get at it. I can't say I was in a very good way back then, even when my sweetheart slept next to me. And I could never have imagined such a great girl sleeping in my bed and me not getting it up. Oh well, I guess she didn't expect it of me in those days. But shit, *I* expected it of me, because I loved her so much, shit, I still love her so much.

'Sweetheart,' I call again in my gentle seduction voice, 'Please don't be angry with me any more, please, please, please.'

And then I hear her over in the bedroom, saying something really softly; she's got a real talent for talking so softly that I go all quiet and calm too. 'No, no,' I say, 'you mustn't worry, I'm staying here, I'm staying here with you until we've got through it all.'

And then she says something else, and I want her to

come out of there at last, I want her to come to me, I've hidden the shotgun especially, I want her to come to me on the sofa with the shotgun hidden underneath it, and then I want us to sit on the sofa and I'll rest my head on her chest and she'll stroke my hair. I let my hair grow especially for her. I'd always trimmed my hair down to a grade one or two. That was to do with the way I'm scared of a lot of people. No, no, it was nothing to do with being scared of spiders. Mind you, what happens when a big spider drops on your head when your hair's so short, almost shaved off? Does it slip right off again or can it hold on better with its long legs than on a full head of hair? 'Take the shotgun, sweetheart, and shoot that giant spider off my head please.'

So now I have a real quiff, like James Dean or Elvis, and I have to say I like it much better than that short stubble on my head. I always used to tell myself, well if one of those people you're so scared of wants to get you one day – and shit, that's happened often enough – where's he going to grab hold of you if you've hardly got any hair on your head? But I'm not scared any more when my sweetheart's around, not even of spiders. 'Please, please, please,' I call, and my voice isn't as gentle and flattering now as I like it to be. That stupid fear's coming back now, and I squat down on the floor, and I crawl over to the sofa, wait a moment, wasn't I just sitting on the sofa? I wish I could crawl under the sofa where my shotgun's hiding. And I take my shotgun out from under the sofa, stroke its cool rifle and the smooth wood, remove the twenty-shot magazine, filled up to the top with black .177 pellets; they'll even break windows and street lamps. I lie on the floor like that for a while, the shotgun next to me, and when I'm lying like this my sweetheart can't see me, I bet, the table's above me and there are all these bottles on it too. Loads of juice and a bottle of vodka, 120 proof. So we've got pure kiwi juice, lemon juice, undiluted, and all this multi-vitamin shite. I've been drinking the lemon juice straight, for days now. Kiwi tastes better, and I only drink the vodka in tiny sips when I can't take it any more. Lemon juice is supposed to get rid of the really bad pressure, that's what they told me, and my sweetheart fetched all the different juices so that the bad pressure wasn't quite so bad. 'Sweetheart,' I call out, pressing my beautiful shotgun up close to me, 'Sweetheart, I'm a walking vitamin C, please, please, please come out here. Please, please, please.' I always say please three times and sometimes four times, because I love her so much and I'm totally helpless if she doesn't come out and stay by my side. But my sweetheart's angry with me and she's hiding out in bed, and I can't understand it because when she was asleep yesterday, I haven't slept for three or four days now, so when she was asleep yesterday and I started out sitting on the bed next to her and watching her sleep, and when she was asleep like that, my God, she looks so beautiful, she looks so gorgeous when she's asleep, the face is . . . no, no, no, why am I saying 'the face', it's her face, and it glows, really glows, her face. And as it's glowing like that with all the lovely blonde hair all around it, I can't help but think of Monroe. I told her that once, that she looks a bit like Monroe, her lips and her nose, but she just laughed and said I was crazy, but I think she knows it herself really and she's proud of it too. Got her hair done the same way, or at least a bit like it. I watched a couple of Monroe films with her to prove it, kept on pressing 'pause' and saying, 'Look, Marilyn Monroe, you and Marilyn Monroe.'

I shove my shotgun back under the sofa; I'm all mixed up, and when I'm mixed up like this my shotgun's no good to me at all, because then stupid stuff happens with me and my shotgun.

Because then I get up and go to the window. With my shotgun. And then I open the window and cock my beautiful shotgun. It goes clack-clack. Then I position the shotgun and aim at the street lamp. And it's not as if it's just any old street lamp; it's one of those disturbing street lamps, one of those lamps that never stop annoying you. And don't anyone try and tell me street lamps don't annoy you. This one annoys the hell out of me. The damn thing's broken. Shines all day even though you can't see it until it gets dark. The street lamps only go on at a certain time, but this damn lamp is totally out of sync, and that doesn't just get me mixed up, it drives me crazy. So the gun's positioned, I take good aim, and then my finger's on the trigger. And then I feel that all I have to do is move my finger slightly so the .177 pellet hits the street lamp. And I don't pull the trigger straight away. I always make the most of the moment before I pull the trigger. Not just with the shotgun and the street lamp. And that's why my sweetheart's mad now and not talking to me and hiding in bed so all I can see is her nose. Oh, that nose. I always want to tweak it, just a little tweak with one finger. Her gorgeous nose could make a nose fetishist of me, though

I don't even know what a nose fetishist does. Honey rose, honey rose with your beautiful nose. I had a woman once, I didn't have her for long, just one night and not even all night long, and in that half or quarter of a night she kept on calling me 'honey', but she probably said that to all the guys, and I have to admit . . . 'Sweetheart,' I call out, 'Sweetheart!' and I've had about enough now.

Yes, I made a mess of things while she was asleep, I have to admit it. I couldn't stick it out. And what does she know about what it's like when you can't stick it out any more? But Jesus, that's no way to behave, hiding under the covers in the bedroom. So I pull the trigger. I only have to move my finger a tiny little bit. And then there's a bang, but not like I was shooting a real carbine, it's just a short, dry pop! – and then there's a fraction of a second before I hear my lovely little .177 projectile hitting the street lamp. But that damn street lamp's a tough one. I can hit it as many times as I want, it just won't break, and it shines and shines and drives me round the bend. The protective glass around the bulb's just too tough, too thick, too solid, too stable, too protective, but then that's what it's there for. So I close the window again. Put the shotgun away, suddenly feel utterly sickened by the shotgun, utterly sickened, starting in my feet and rising incredibly fast, so fast that I only just manage to wrench the window open, lean over and puke out of it. I hear it slapping onto the pavement, and I wish I could puke in a curve high enough to hit the street lamp. I wipe a hand across my chin. Smells of lemons. And now the lemon smell rises slowly from below, and I close the window again quickly.

She's crying. She's crying softly in the bedroom, heard me shooting and puking. She cries so softly I can hardly hear it. She's actually very strong, or she'd long since have given up on me, long since have chucked me out, and I'd be sitting back in my little one-room flat. And it wouldn't end well there, oh no, never. But it's all ended well now, I believe that, I believe that so firmly it almost hurts. I wouldn't make it without her though, and it's doing my head in that she's crying because of me now, because I've been so weak again and I'd promised her never to be weak again, and all the juice she got for me, and all the pills, garlic capsules, hawthorn, ginseng, valerian (high-dose), St John's wort, as if all that shite could do me much good, but she said it'd help me, so I want it to help me, and it's doing my head in that she's crying because of me now. And I want to go to her and tell her she doesn't have to cry any more because of me and I'll never be weak again, really and truly, honestly. But my shirt's covered in puke and I'm so scared she'll send me away if I sit down next to her. Or that she won't say anything at all, that'd be even worse – me sitting there next to her and her not saying a word, and the tears, it breaks my heart to see tears in her eyes. Marilyn Monroe should always be smiling. And I go to the table where all the packets of pills are scattered between all the bottles. A sip of vodka, just a tiny sip, I've earned it now, haven't I? It's just as a disinfectant really, because of the puke. I screw the cap off the bottle, but before I drink I take a few of the pills and put them on the palm of my hand. 'Sweetheart,' I call out, 'I'm taking your healthy pills!'

Three of the green garlic capsules, no, better take six, a

double dose. Two long red hawthorn capsules, they're good for my circulation, regulate my blood pressure, the garlic does that too but hawthorn improves blood flow to the heart muscle, and I need a strong heart so I don't go back to my shoes again. In my shoes, out in the hall. I've hidden something in there under the orthopaedic insole, it's a sort of emergency supply, but I don't need it any more, I'll chuck it down the toilet later and flush it away, but actually an emergency supply's only for a real emergency, and I'm sure that won't happen now, and if it does I'll stick it out, so I might as well just leave the stuff in my shoe. You should never throw away emergency supplies, and certainly not flush them down the toilet. It's a pretty clever hiding place and all, under my sweaty insole.

And the way she searched me, turned every pocket inside out, patted down my shirts with both hands – but she never thought of my shoes. I'm proud of that hiding place and I add three ginseng capsules to the other pills in my palm. So now I've got six garlic, two hawthorn and three ginseng capsules. Isn't there a joke about impotence, how you're supposed to tie a ginseng root to your dick or something, but I don't think that's why my sweetheart got me the ginseng capsules. I've been taking the stuff for days now though, and when we've got through all this I'll spend a whole day and a night in bed with her. I'll make us a baby, oh yes, how often have I dreamt about the two of us having kids? And she has too, I know she has, she wrote to me when I . . . No, no, don't think about it, don't think about the toilet brush, toilet brush, toilet brush, what are those bastards doing with the toilet brush . . . ? So one of these extra-large valerian capsules as well then, they used to take valerian root in the old days for heart palpitations, St John's wort. 'Sweetheart,' I shout, my voice almost cracking, 'I'm taking all your healthy medicine!'

And then I stuff all the tablets on my palm, a proper tower, into my mouth; a couple of them fall out again, I swallow and retch, swallow and retch and put the vodka to my lips and feel like someone's ramming their fist into my oesophagus. The toilet brush, the toilet brush, take the fucking toilet brush away. I scream, high and shrill, and there are tablets stuck to my lips and my chin, and I feel the vodka wetting my shirt. There's a knock and a ring at the door. And I turn around in circles a couple of times, drop the bottle, a terrible crashing and smashing, I don't stop turning in circles, the bottle must have fallen on the table and knocked over all the other bottles of healthy juice. And I turn around and around until I fall over, I'm lying on the floor, I want to crawl to my shotgun, want to crawl to my shoes, didn't I crawl to my shoes a while ago? Then I want to crawl into the bedroom and lie down with her. But there's a knocking and ringing at the door, no, I haven't been to my shoes for hours, since yesterday, since forever, since my sweetheart got so mad and sad at me I haven't been to my shoes, and I know that now for sure, because now it's not just knocking and ringing at the door, it's knocking and ringing inside me too. I beat both fists against my chest and scream, 'Stop, stop, stop,' and now I feel like I'm bathing in hot water, almost boiling hot, bathing in a huge saucepan that's bubbling and simmering all around me now, and I know the only thing that can save me now is my shoes, but how am I supposed to get out of the boiler and out of the water to my shoes? There's that story about the cooks in the canteen who used to bathe in the soup kettles, but I never believed it. My mother used to tell me it sometimes, she worked in a canteen as well, but now I believe her, believe every word of it, because that's what I feel like, as if I was being boiled to death in a huge soup kettle. The lid's fallen closed, and when the lid closes the kettle heats up automatically – the soup doesn't want to get out and doesn't scream and shout when it's done. I'm screaming and shouting, there's a crashing and splintering, and I don't know why I'm bleeding, but then I'm suddenly perfectly still, I give it all up, I'm perfectly light and I can't feel my scalded skin any more. I go out into the hallway, walk to the door; I'm so light I think I'm floating. But the door's open already, and I'm floating around between the cops. The cops shove me and hold me, drag me across the hall back into the living room, see my shotgun, one of the cops takes my shotgun, and then I'm in the bedroom with them. 'Leave her alone,' I say. 'She's got nothing to do with it, just leave her alone, please.' But they don't leave her alone – they pull the cover off her. And I hit out all around me; I want to launch myself on the cops but they hold me tight.

She's naked, and her skin's so white I close my eyes for a moment. The cops say something but I take no notice, I just look at her lying there so still in front of me. Her hair's fallen over her face so I can't see her eyes. What I see is my hands round her neck. The marks of my hands.

They lead me out of the bedroom, my arms behind my back. It's dark in the living room, broken glass crunches under my feet, and as they shove me into the hall I turn around one more time.

Outside the window, in the light of the street lamp, Mary Monroe smiles at me.

FATTY LOVES

She was very shy. She always looked down at the floor when she came up to the blackboard. An eleven-year-old girl with brown hair down to her shoulders. Year five. Sometimes she wore her hair in a short ponytail. She was slightly pale. A long school year, year five. Later she turned twelve. That was after the summer holidays, at the start of year six. He still remembered her birthday very clearly. The way her friends had whispered and laughed as he stood at the garden gate and waved at her. He'd been sweating, and his face must have been bright red, like it always was when he sweated. She'd smiled and raised her hand briefly and then looked down at the ground. She was very shy. She raised her top lip slightly when she smiled and he saw her front teeth. The two in the middle were a tiny bit longer than the ones next to them, but just a tiny bit. And when she thought about things and got annoyed, all the numbers, that small crease ran from the top of her nose to her forehead.

He thought of all this often, imagining it, especially when he was alone and eating, and he ate a lot and was usually alone. Always, actually. He was eating a whole salami. Now he put it aside; the pain was back in his left arm, starting in his chest, aching, getting stronger, so strong that his breath came short and he felt dizzy. He laid the salami carefully on the plate, alongside a thick pork cutlet in aspic and three slices of bread and butter. He walked around the kitchen, massaging his left arm and then his chest, went to the door, saw the dark, long hallway ahead of him, the white doors, bedroom, living room, and went back to the table. He sat down, his belly brushing against the table, and the plate and the teapot and the glass gave a slight rattle. He'd hardly drunk any coffee since the stabbing and aching in his left arm and chest had started to come more and more often. He'd been meaning to go to the doctor for weeks, but he barely left the house now.

The last time he'd been out for a walk, a couple of days ago, he'd stopped at that garden gate. It was a small block of flats but it was a couple of years now since she'd lived there. She was nearly twenty-one now; it would be her birthday in twelve days. He'd leaned on the garden gate, and although it was quite cool – the entire summer had been cool and rainy – he'd broken out in a sweat. She had tied up her brown hair in two little bunches. A brightly coloured party dress. Balloons in the trees. Her parents had been sitting at a table, and he stood at the garden gate, stood there a good while and hoped they might invite him in for a cup of coffee and a piece of cake. But they hadn't even said hello, even though they'd seen him. He waved at her again, and she smiled, then turned around and ran to her friends, who looked over at him and whispered and laughed. He turned away and left. The bag with the teddy in it knocked against his leg as he walked. The teddy was holding a calculator in both hands. The teddy had been quite expensive; the calculator was a new model. The calculator teddy was wearing a mortarboard and large spectacles. Its shirt was decorated with numbers; it didn't have any trousers. It had small plastic rods on its hands where you could push the calculator in and out again. He'd given her the teddy later, after class. 'Could you stay behind for a minute please,' he'd said to her, 'I want to have a word with you about the last test.' She hadn't done particularly well in the last test, even though she'd often stayed behind after class for extra tuition. There were four in the group: three boys and her. Sometimes they'd done more practice on their own after that, once the others had gone, twenty or thirty minutes, or longer. She was really good at German and most other subjects, among the best in the class, but maths . . . And he did everything he could for her, to help her understand numbers and learn to like them. He loved numbers.

'Here, for you.' He put the calculator teddy on the table in front of her. 'Happy Birthday.' She reached hesitantly for the teddy and pulled it slightly closer to her. 'Belated best wishes,' he said, 'Happy Birthday, Juliana.'

'For me?' she said, smiling and raising her top lip slightly and looking down at the table. Then she lifted her head, looked at him and said, 'Thank you, thanks.'

He sat down on the little chair next to her, his belly brushing against the table. 'Imagine we're in a florist's,' he said, 'and you buy yourself seven lovely flowers, and they cost . . .' he thought for a moment, 'they cost seventeen marks fifty.' 'What kind of flowers, Mr Krein?' she asked, still holding the teddy tight in one hand. He thought again. 'Roses,' he said. 'No, lilies.' The exercise was in the textbook and it said roses there, seven roses, but he wanted her to buy herself lilies, even though he knew nothing about flowers. 'Why are lilies so expensive?' she asked.

'They're,' he said, 'they're especially beautiful lilies, special lilies,' and she nodded. 'So, one lily,' he said, 'how much does one lily cost?'

She took the calculator, removing it carefully from the teddy's hands, and he said, 'No, wait a moment. Write it down first and work it out, and then you can check it.'

She put the calculator aside, picked up her fountain pen and bent over her exercise book. 'Seven lilies,' she said softly. 'Seventeen marks fifty,' he said, leaning over to her. 'And how much does one cost?' He saw her writing the numbers in the little squares. He saw the small crease running from the top of her nose to her forehead.

Sweat ran down his face, and then the stabbing and aching was back again, from his chest to his left arm, and he held onto the garden gate for support. 'Juliana,' he said. Her friends called her 'Juli' – like the month. The school holidays were in July, the long summer holidays. He held onto the garden gate for support, with both hands. Then he closed his eyes and waited. He opened his eyes and saw the plate of food in front of him. 'Happy Birthday, Juli,' he said. But then he noticed that no time had passed, that he was still sitting at the table, with the same salami, the same cutlet in aspic shining in the light falling through the kitchen window. He ate salami and pork cutlet in aspic every evening; he hardly left the house now and he often thought of her birthday, the closer it came. Did she have a boyfriend, he wondered. Probably, she was almost twenty-one after all. But she'd always been so shy. Had always looked so shyly down at the floor when she came up to the blackboard. Perhaps she had a child already, a small child. He banged on the table, swept his open palm across the table. The plate fell on the floor and shattered, the salami bounced across the tiles, he had a nice tiled kitchen and the cutlet in aspic slapped onto the tiles with a dry splat and stayed put as if it were stuck to the floor.

He lowered his head carefully onto the tabletop. He was fifty-four and he was never going to have children. He stayed like that for a while, resting his arms on his belly and folding his hands together. 'If I become a father at the age of fifty-five, and my daughter has a son at twenty-three, how old would I have to be for my five-year-old grandson . . .' He fell silent. Even numbers brought him no pleasure any more. There was no one there any more to whom he could explain the magic of numbers. And there hadn't been for a long time now. 'Five to the power of four,' he said. 'That's five times five times five times five. The small number controls the big one.' He took her hand. 'Count it on your fingers, go ahead. One times five, times five for the second time, times five for the third time, times five for the fourth time.'

She counted. 'The small number controls the big one,' she said, and he looked at the crease above her nose, 'five to the power of two is twenty-five, that's easy, five to the power of three is twenty-five times two.'

'No,' he said with a tap at her fingers, 'the five for the third time, twenty-five times five. It's like,' he thought for a moment, 'when you skim a stone, skim a flat stone across water, Juli, and it bounces off four times before it goes under. You can skim stones, can't you, Juli?'

'On the water,' she said. He stood with her by the water, the lake outside town, the motorway beyond the embankment; they heard the hum of all the cars. She stood in front of him in her brightly coloured dress, the one she'd be wearing on her birthday, skimming flat stones across the water. 'Seventy-five,' she said, 'seventy-five times five.' He was wearing a loose Hawaiian shirt, watching her skim the stones across the water, and he was happy.

He walked slowly down the hallway, the white bathroom door ahead of him. He ran a hand over his face. He hadn't shaved for a few days. Back then he'd shaved every morning and moisturised his face and gone to school with a smooth, shiny face. He'd usually started to sweat on the bus. Then he'd sat sweating in the staff room, his sandwiches and coffee on the table in front of him.

They talked about him behind his back; he knew that. Mrs Koch and Mrs Bräuninger put their heads together, Mrs Bräuninger with her silver whistle on a string round her neck all the time; he'd often stood by the window and looked out at the sports field, looking for Juli and hearing Mrs

Bräuninger's whistle. Juli was very good at sports, always a front-runner in races, and she won almost every sprint. She was wearing a pale blue tracksuit. She ran across the playing field to the other girls. She was laughing – he could see that from up here. He even thought he could see her teeth. He leaned against the windowsill and listened to the class behind him writing, the rustle of paper, the scratching of pens, now and then soft whispers. She didn't have maths on Wednesdays, but when he taught 7b at noon he could look down at the playing field, if the weather was good. In the winter and when it rained she was in the gym with the others. Sometimes the girls and Mrs Bräuninger didn't come out even though the weather was good; they played volleyball in the gym or did gymnastics and did all the things he'd never been able to do and had always hated as a child. He'd been bad at sports, fat and heavy-breathing, and when he thought about how they'd laughed at him when he clung onto the climbing bar and didn't move an inch upwards, he wished he could clear the memories from his brain like old results on a calculator – 'Fatty, fatty' – he thought about numbers, about fractions, quadratic equations, matrix equations. He looked down at the playing field and looked for her in the group of girls, two or three pale blue tracksuits – there she was; he recognised her brown hair, which she tied up in a short ponytail. Eleven years, exactly a quarter of his life. Eleven years ago he'd been at a different school, in a different town. The German and Music teacher – a small, delicate woman. He thought about interior and exterior angles, about the first thirty-five digits of pi, about straight lines that would meet somewhere in infinity, but at night he dreamed of Miss Kerner, German and Music, and woke up sweating, and imagined inviting her to dinner, imagined himself calculating food and drinks, aperitifs and desserts and champagne in his head quick as a flash, then they'd sit on the sofa in his living room, close together, he'd explain the infinity of numbers and Miss Kerner would recite a poem.

Thirty-three, eleven, forty-four years. A series that almost fit together. He leaned against the windowsill and saw Juli among all the other girls, lining up in several queues, raising their arms and moving their torsos, Mrs Bräuninger in front of them, the silver whistle in her mouth. He had invited Miss Kerner to dinner back then, but she'd just smiled and said, 'How nice, thank you,' and told him she couldn't come. Somehow, even the pupils had got wind of his rejected invitation, odd nasty remarks now and then, 'K and K, Kerner and Krein,' his colleagues smiled about him and in his mind he drew huge circles, with a giant set of compasses, huge intersecting circles, and he had to calculate the area of the cross section. And now they were whispering behind his back again after so many years, a different school, a different town, gossiping in the staff room, 'Fatty and Juliana, something's not right there,' and he saw her down there on the playing field, and when she raised her hands above her head she seemed to be waving at him.

He stood in his living room, not knowing how long he'd been standing there, not quite knowing what day it was, not quite knowing what time it was, still seeing Juli, her light blue tracksuit getting paler and paler, and he shook his head. He looked over to the window; it was still light outside. It was summer and the days were still long. Then he remembered the cutlet in aspic that had splatted onto the kitchen floor, and suddenly he knew there were exactly eight days to go until her twenty-first birthday. And then he knew why he was standing in the living room in front of his cabinet. He took a couple of steps towards it, turned the key and opened the small glass door. The class photograph and the dog made out of conkers. Ever since he'd stopped taking the bus to school, he'd often stood in front of the cabinet in the morning – he still woke up at the same time – and looked at the dog and the photo through the glass, not opening the little door. She was in the last row at the back. She was smiling. He picked up the photo, for the first time in years; he had to squint and hold it right up to his face – he must need glasses. She was smiling. He was standing to one side. His bald head was shining and he was red in the face. 'My dear Mr Krein,' the headmaster said, 'my dear Mr Krein, you've been teaching your syllabus very well for years, you've been popular for years with your colleagues and pupils,' the headmaster hesitated, probably aware that wasn't quite true. 'My dear Mr Krein,' he started in again, and Mr Krein interrupted him – even years later he was amazed at his courage, but actually it hadn't been courage, it was sadness, the onset of sadness, for he knew what was coming. 'Please stop all this "My dear Mr Krein" business,' said Mr Krein. 'Just get to the point and stop it, will you just stop it . . .' Then he almost shouted, 'Get to the point, will you, for God's sake!'

The headmaster flinched, leaning forward so their

heads were almost touching. 'It's about the thing with the girl, Juliana. Her parents came to see me. Do you know what you're getting yourself into?'

'I'm not getting myself into anything,' said Mr Krein softly. 'I'm not getting into anything at all.'

He put the photo back in the cabinet and reached for the conker dog. As he stretched out his arm the pain came back, but he took no notice. He held onto the dog with both hands, took a few steps back and dropped down onto the sofa. Four times they had sat here. The textbooks and her exercise book in front of them on the table. A large bottle of juice and a bar of chocolate. She took the dog made out of conkers out of her satchel and put it on the table between the books and the juice and the chocolate. 'I made this for you,' she said. A little animal made of conkers and matchsticks. He hadn't realised right away that it was supposed to be a dog; it could have been a sheep or a cat, but then she'd said, 'It's a dachshund, Mr Krein, for you.'

'Thank you, Juli,' he said. 'I've always wanted a dachshund.'

She smiled, and he took the conker dachshund, balanced it on his belly and cautiously stroked the large conker that was its head. 'My parents,' said Juli, and he said, 'Yes?' but he wasn't listening, he was stroking the dachshund moving up and down on his belly as he breathed. She talked, and he closed his eyes and saw three circles, two large and one small between the two large ones. The two large circles touched in the middle of the small circle, then they moved apart again, and it looked like they were holding the small circle tight in the middle. 'I'm going now,' she said. She stood in front of him, pressing her exercise book to her chest and her chin. 'Bye, Mr Krein.' The dog fell off his stomach as he reached a hand out for her. 'Stay a bit longer, Juli, I'll take you home.'

'No.' She pushed the exercise book higher, until it touched the tip of her nose, and spoke through the paper. 'My parents, Mr Krein . . .'

The dachshund was lying on the floor at his feet. He bent down and balanced it on its short matchstick legs. A stabbing pain in his head. He took a deep breath as he leaned back. 'Is there a law against going for an ice cream with Juli? Is there a law against going swimming with Juli? Is there a law against . . . ?' He started shouting but there was no one there, only the dachshund at his feet. He had shouted when the man from the school inspection board had sat opposite him in the secretary's office. 'Investigations, you go ahead and do your investigations!'

'At the moment all it's about is unjustified favouritism and support for a pupil . . .'

He stood in front of the mirror in his bathroom, pressing both hands to the glass. How did that little poem go again, the one she'd recited for him when they were sitting in the sun? That May had been so warm . . . two ice cream sundaes. He saw her lips moving, her hands gesticulating above her ice cream while she recited the poem. She closed her eyes when she got stuck, the small crease from the top of her nose to her forehead. Was it Goethe? He knew nothing about literature. Yes, it was Goethe. Or maybe Schiller or some other poet? He'd been so happy, next to her at the table, and her hands above the ice cream sundaes, and the poem, but the only thing he was good at remembering was numbers. 'My heart it beat . . .'

He took his hands off the mirror, saw the moist prints they left behind fading. '. . . the evening bowed t'ward the earth . . .' The blackboard . . . He shuddered, didn't want that in his head, the blackboard, the big white letters; he went to the door. He walked back down the dark hallway to the kitchen.

He stood on the tiles, feeling for the light switch. He looked over at the window; it must be evening by now. He turned on the light and took a couple of steps, then his legs fell away beneath him, he raised both arms, nothing to hold onto, then he was on the floor, and his head smashed against the wall. He lay on his back like that for a while, then slowly turned onto his side. The trampled cutlet in aspic lay next to him.

He went into the classroom. He went to the blackboard, not looking around, heard the children talking softly, the rustle of paper; he opened the two flaps of the blackboard. 'Fatty loves Juli,' it said in wobbly white capital letters, a heart drawn beneath it in red chalk. He placed one hand on either side of the heart and stood like that for a while, supporting himself against the blackboard, all quiet behind him now. He stood upright, saw the moist prints left behind by his hands – he could make out each separate finger – then he turned around slowly. Juli's seat was empty. He went to the door.

He walked down the hallway. He was sweating, and the sweat ran into his eyes.

OF DOGS AND HORSES

It started when his dog suddenly started to limp, and then came to a halt outright. It was a pretty big dog, a Rottweiler-Doberman mix, a hundred pounds, and in the six years that Rolf had been living with him the dog had never limped and had never just stopped walking either. He'd been with him in the mountains and by the sea, took long walks with him every day, and the dog's long ears moved up and down when he ran.

'Piet,' said Rolf, 'what's up with you, boy, you're not that old yet.' Piet stood in the middle of the pavement, his back legs far apart; he stood there as if straddling something, looking at him with his dark eyes. He pulled on the leash but the dog didn't move. He squatted down in front of him and stroked his head. 'What's up, boy, what's the matter, shall we just have a bit of a rest? You'll be all right in a minute, won't you Piet?'

He'd called his dog Piet because of Pete Sampras, the tennis player, but he'd written the name with an 'ie' on the

dog licence to make it a bit more mysterious. Rolf wasn't really a tennis fan at all, but he'd seen Pete Sampras a couple of
times on TV in some tournament or other, and the elegance
with which he outplayed his opponents had impressed him.
And now Piet was standing there and wouldn't budge an
inch and hung his head. They were still a mile or so away
from home and he wouldn't be able to carry him. He'd lifted
him up for fun a couple of times and lugged him around the
apartment, but the dog had wriggled around and his back
had started aching after only a few yards.

He gave another tug on the leash and said, 'Come on,
let's go home, there'll be a treat for you when we get home.'
And the dog took a few steps; his back legs buckled strangely
inwards and he limped a little, but he was walking. They
walked home very slowly, and sometimes Piet stopped again,
and then he stroked him and waited until he could carry
on. They lived on the first floor, up half a flight of stairs, and
the dog had problems getting up the couple of steps to the
apartment door; that morning when they came back from
their first walk of the day there had been no stopping him;
he knew his food was inside.

He opened the front door and Piet went straight to his
corner and lay down. 'Damn it,' he said, 'what on earth's up
with you boy, you're not gonna . . .' He sat down in the arm-
chair right in front of the dog's blanket. He often sat here
and read the newspaper or watched TV, his dog right next to
him. All he had to do was reach out his hand to touch him.

'You're not gonna give up on me,' he said, putting his
hand on Piet's head and stroking him behind the ears. 'You

can't give up on me.' He sat in the chair and looked down at Piet, who lay quite still, only his back rising and falling slightly. It was very quiet in the flat, with only the fridge humming in the kitchen, and he sat there and took his hand off Piet's head, folded his hands and rubbed them together over and over. They had been living together for six years, Rolf and Piet, and he couldn't imagine sitting alone in his flat again, like eight years ago when his wife had gone, just the humming of the fridge in the silence. He rubbed his hands together, then jumped up and ran to the kitchen. He fetched the big pack of dog biscuits out of the cupboard and took out a handful. Usually the sound of the cupboard doors banging was enough to make Piet come running, but he didn't come even when he shook the pack. He put it back in the cupboard and stood in the kitchen with the handful of dog biscuits, waiting. The fridge hummed next to him, and because he couldn't stand it any more he shouted, 'Piet, where are you boy, I've got a treat for you!' And then Rolf heard him. He heard the tip-tap of his steps in the hall, and then he saw Piet's head in the doorway, 'Come on, come and get it,' and the dog ran towards him, jumped up at him, and he said, 'Down boy, sit,' and Piet sat down in front of him and stretched out a paw towards him, although he hadn't said 'Shake', and then he gave him the dog biscuits and Piet crunched them up and ate them, and he said, 'There you are boy, you're eating them up nicely, you're not feeling so bad are you, you were just tired before.' He watched as Piet ate the dog biscuits one after another, and he was happy.

'Hip dysplasia,' said the veterinarian and pointed to the

X-rays, but Rolf couldn't make out anything much on them. 'Advanced stage,' said the vet, 'we'd have to operate. There are various options, gold implants and so on, but with artificial joints and the latest methods he could live a long life.'

'He was running around just two days ago.' Piet lay next to him, and Rolf kept his hand on his head. Piet was really scared of the vet, he moaned and yelped in the waiting room and didn't want to come through to the surgery, although he only had his injections there once a year. He could smell the other animals' fear, and maybe death too.

'Hereditary,' said the vet, 'nothing you can do.' He had given Piet a mild anaesthetic shot so they could X-ray him better, and then injected a contrast agent into his joints.

'Dogs don't show it right away when they're in pain,' said the vet. 'They don't know what it is, where it's coming from. Not until they can't keep going any more.'

Piet was asleep, and the vet and the nurse wanted to lift him onto the X-ray machine, but he had said, 'No, I'll do that,' and squatted down, put his arms around him and lifted him up.

'With painkillers,' said the vet, 'he'll keep going for a while . . . if you take really good care of him . . .'

'And then?' He still had his hand on Piet's head. Piet had woken up from the anaesthetic a while ago, but he was still very weak and lay there next to him, and Rolf felt him breathing.

'It'd be OK for a year or two,' said the vet, 'maybe longer, but at some point he'd just be suffering. If you don't want to go through with the operation . . .'

They took a taxi home. Now and then Rolf turned around to him, but Piet was lying at the back of the cab and was still pretty knocked out, although back when Rolf had still had a car and they would go for a drive together he was uneasy all the way, moaning and yelping.

'It's nothing serious, is it?' said the driver.

'No, just a routine check-up.' Rolf hadn't taken a taxi for years. He couldn't really afford it either, the examination and the tablets had used up almost all his money. He could have asked his brother to pick them up from the vet's, but he didn't want to talk to his brother right now; he'd have to talk to him later about the operation, but he was scared. His brother didn't much like Piet, and Piet didn't much like his brother either. He growled at him and sometimes started barking when his brother came by. But his brother didn't come by too often. 'Nice dog you've got there,' said the driver.

'Yes, he is.' He turned around to Piet again, who was licking at his hips with his long pink tongue now, at the place where the vet had injected the contrast agent. 'A Rottweiler, isn't he?'

'Rottweiler-Doberman.'

'Really nice animal,' said the driver and nodded and looked at Piet in the rear-view mirror. And Rolf looked in the mirror too and saw his dog's big head and felt very proud.

Rolf had been playing the lottery for years but he had only won once. Over four hundred deutschmarks with a special system using ten numbers in different combinations. He had had three lots of four numbers come up and five lots of three with his system, and they had brought him over four hundred deutschmarks in winnings. If five of his numbers had come up (which he always dreamed of; he never actually expected six), maybe even two fives would have turned up in his system, and that would have brought him big bucks, but still, the four hundred marks had been a lot of money for him at the time, even though he was still in work back then.

He didn't play the system any more because it had cost him twenty marks every week, and after they switched to the euro and he lost his job, forty euros a month was just too much for him.

Now he handed in just one set of six crossed-off numbers every Saturday afternoon, always number four because of the four letters in their names, Piet and Rolf, and five other numbers he had picked for no special reason. But he never won anything, and he didn't know anyone who had won big money on the lottery.

And big money was what he needed. Three thousand euros was big money to Rolf.

'If it wasn't for Piet,' his brother had said, 'maybe. But just so you can patch up that dilapidated old dog . . .'

'Piet isn't dilapidated.'

'Three thousand euros, Jesus, d'you think I'm made of money?'

'You've got more than me at any rate. Don't you get it, it's the latest surgery, he can live a long . . .'

'Listen, Rolf, I can't help it that you lost your job. And you know that back when Martha went, I . . .'

'No,' he said, 'it's nothing to do with her, it's about Piet.'

'Jesus, if he's so sick why don't you have him . . .'

He had left without another word. He had walked the streets and thought about who else he could ask, who he even knew who had that kind of money. Then he'd gone back home, laid down next to Piet on the rug. He only went on short walks with him now, and Piet had started to limp again despite the tablets. Rolf lay next to him, one hand on his back, feeling him breathing, and they lay together until it got dark and he got up and turned on the light.

He took a short walk with Piet, and once the dog had disappeared into the bushes and taken a crap he took him home again. There was lots of dog shit on the pavements in his area, and he was proud that not a single turd was from Piet. He had taught him when he was very small only to shit in bushes and on the grass.

'I'll be back soon, boy, look after the place, be good.'

Piet lay in his corner and looked at him; whenever Rolf left the house he looked at him with his dark eyes. He didn't like being alone, like all dogs. Whenever Rolf had to go out for a while longer he told the old lady next door; she liked Piet and was happy to keep an eye on him. She was on her own too and Piet liked her. She was over seventy and Rolf was scared she'd die one day; there was no one else to look after Piet when he had to go away. But now he just wanted to walk and think and maybe have a drink; he had enough money for that. He threw Piet a big dog biscuit and could still hear him crunching as he locked the door.

He walked the streets, not knowing where he wanted to go, walked past the bars and kebab shops, wanted to think, about the money, about the operation, but he was tired and he walked very slowly, and he knew there was nobody who would help him. He drank two small bottles of beer at a snack bar that stayed open until late at night. He was the only customer; the owner leaned on the counter, drinking coffee and watching the people going by his little place. Rolf drank a shot and paid his bill, then he too went on his way.

On a corner was a new place that he didn't know yet. A large neon sign with red letters: 'Sports Bets', and there were pictures in the window of football players, boxers, and a big horse galloping along with a jockey wearing a cap, bent low over the horse's back and seeming to fuse with the horse. A couple of men came out of the door, talking loudly and waving little slips of paper; not money, he could tell. They walked along the road bellowing and laughing, then disappeared around the corner. Rolf stayed where he was and looked at the pictures and the sign, then he turned around and went home.

Standing in the bookmakers the next day, he was surprised at how large it was and how many people were standing around him, looking at all the monitors on the walls. It was Saturday, after three in the afternoon, and most of the screens were showing football, but on some of them there were horses galloping, and a couple of men were standing there, holding slips and newspapers and staring at the horses. They didn't talk and didn't seem to care about the noise all around them. 'Kick the damn thing,' shouted a man next to him, punching the air, 'What's the matter with you, even I could've scored ...'

'Yeah!' growled a man in front of another monitor, 'That's it, I've got it,' and Rolf walked slowly over to the silent men and the horses. But they weren't as quiet any more now, the race seemed to be entering the final phase, and they twitched their nervous shoulders, stepping from one leg to the other and whispering things like, 'Go on, come on,' 'Five, what do I care about number five,' 'Yeah, yeah, yeah,' 'He's losing it, he's gonna eat dust,' and then they got slightly louder, and then the race was over. Rolf was standing right behind them; some of them took their slips to the long counter, where there were already lots of people fiddling with slips and money, giving them to the men behind the counter; there were a couple of women too, taking the bets and the money, but otherwise he couldn't see any women in the room; actually, no, over there were two old ladies huddled together, studying a newspaper spread out in front of them.

Rolf went closer to the monitor, where numbers and the names of the horses now appeared. Star King, he read, and then a man making notes on his paper pushed in front of him. 'How much d'you think the triple was worth?'

'Star King had over fifteen to win, the places weren't bad either, not everyone saw that coming. It'll be a nice little earner.'

'Real nice,' said another man, 'six or seven hundred for the trifecta, I reckon, at least.'

'I had Prairie Louise down,' said a short man with a grey beard, who was filling out a betting slip against the wall next to the monitor, 'she had good odds and all.'

'Yeah, six to one's not bad, she was doing all right until the finishing straight.' They talked about the race just run and the next one, filling out betting slips and flicking through their newspapers, and Rolf stood between them, not knowing what all the numbers and words meant, only understanding one thing: 'Six or seven hundred at least.'

'The payouts,' said the short man with the beard, 'the payouts should be up in a minute.' They formed a semi-circle around the monitor, and then a few numbers appeared again, and the short man with the beard shouted, 'Eight hundred and seventy-three to one, Jesus, even five euros would have made you a packet.'

'And nearly nine thousand for ten euros,' another man said, 'I should've risked it, but hell, who'd have guessed it, Star King to win and Miss Marmalade and One Night Girl placed, you might as well play the lottery!' They laughed and flicked through their papers, and the bearded man took his betting slip up to the counter.

'Eight thousand seven hundred and thirty,' Rolf said over and over on the way home, 'eight thousand seven hundred and thirty.' Ten horses had run, he had understood that much. Picking three horses correctly out of ten seemed more likely than waiting for five numbers to come up in the lottery. And there must be combinations where you didn't have to bet on the exact order of the horses. He'd been to the races as a child once with his grandmother, but all he could remember was the jockeys' bright silks, which seemed to blend together into a long stream of colour as they galloped past him on their horses.

He had no idea about horse races and betting, but an old friend of his had spent a lot of time at the racetrack in the old East German days and up to the mid nineties, and had told him a good deal about it. And he thought he remembered that this old friend, who he hadn't seen for almost ten years, had won a stack of money. And as he walked home now, past the bars and kebab shops and the snack bar where he'd drunk two beers and a shot last night, he knew this was his last chance. Piet and Rolf and the horses.

'You haven't been round for ages, Rolf.'

He hadn't said 'Hello' or 'How's it going?' or 'What do you want?' – he'd just opened the door, stared at him a while, and now he said it again in the same low voice: 'You haven't been round for ages, Rolf.'

'No,' said Rolf. 'Time flies, Schäfer.' They stood like that for a while, Rolf outside the apartment, Schäfer in the half-open door, looking at each other in silence, until the light went out on the stairs and Schäfer said, 'If you want to come in . . .'

'Yes, thanks.' He walked behind him along the corridor, which was completely empty apart from a pair of shoes on a large mat. Schäfer opened a door, and they walked into a room that was just as empty, nothing but a table and two chairs, and a picture hanging on the wall; it looked like a real oil painting, a brown horse and a white horse galloping with their riders through green, hilly countryside.

'Take a seat.'

'Thanks.' They sat down at the table, and Rolf held up

the cloth bag he'd brought with him. 'Brought you a little present.' He pulled out the bottle of Goldkrone brandy and put it on the table.

'Only the best, eh Rolf?' He got up and went out of the room. Rolf listened but he couldn't hear anything, no banging of cupboard doors, no clinking. Then Schäfer came back with two water glasses. 'Been a long time since we last drank together.'

'Sure has,' said Rolf.

Schäfer screwed off the cap and half-filled the two glasses. 'Well then, cheers, here's to seeing you again.'

'Here's to getting together again,' said Rolf; they raised their glasses and drank. Rolf turned his head a couple of times as he drank, but there really was nothing else in the room but the table and the chairs and the picture. There was no ashtray on the table, even though Schäfer had used to smoke like a chimney.

'How are you?' Schäfer was still holding his glass in his hand and turning it; he didn't stop turning it.

'All right thanks,' said Rolf, 'and yourself?'

Schäfer laughed, turned his glass a while longer, then put it down on the table.

'Great, Rolf, just great.'

Rolf nodded and looked at the table, then picked up the bottle. 'Did you know Goldkrone's only twenty-eight percent now? Not thirty-two like in the old days. Because of tax, you know, so it counts as a liqueur. That's what I heard anyway.' He filled the glasses halfway again.

'Hmm,' said Schäfer, 'interesting. A lot of things have

changed.' They drank. They'd often sat together and drunk and talked in the old days.

'Heard about your wife,' said Schäfer, 'sorry to hear that.'

'Thanks. It's ages ago now. I've got a dog now. It's not the same but I'm not on my own.'

'Hmm,' said Schäfer, 'a dog's a fine thing.'

'Shall we have another?'

'Sure. Why not?' They drank. Outside it turned slowly dark; Rolf looked up at the window and saw the red of the twilight above the buildings. 'And you,' he pointed at the picture, 'still at it, still good old Horses Schäfer?'

Schäfer didn't reply, picked up the empty glass again and turned it. He turned it on the tabletop, and they didn't talk and didn't look at each other, and the only sound was the empty glass turning on the table. Then he let go of the glass and stood up. 'It'll be night soon,' he said, 'you came late.' He went to the door and switched on the light. Then he went over to the wall with the picture. 'It's a real Emil Volkers. Worth a bit of money. 1892, that's the year. Bought it over ten years ago from a dealer. He was always at the track – Hoppegarten, outside Berlin. Lost so much he nearly went bust. I was doing good business back then, bought it off him for a good price. That's all I've got now.'

He stood in front of the picture, his back to Rolf, and didn't move, just stood there and looked at it, his arms crossed. Rolf poured himself a splash of Goldkrone, leaned back and drank. Then he started turning the empty glass on the tabletop.

'It's a nice picture, isn't it?' said Schäfer.

'Beautiful.' Rolf looked past Schäfer at the green hills and the two horses. The riders were sitting very upright in their saddles, not like the jockey in the picture on the book-makers' window, who leaned low over the back of the horse.

'Yeah, it's beautiful. But it's wrong. The picture's paint-ed wrong. No human eye can make out the movements of the horses' front and rear legs when they're galloping.'

Schäfer came back to the table, slowly, and picked up his glass. It was empty; Rolf topped it up. Schäfer stood at the table and pointed the glass at the picture. 'The dream gallop phase. You ever heard of it?'

'No,' said Rolf. Schäfer drank. 'You see the front legs, the way they're reaching out far and high. Powerful, aren't they? Looks really elegant. Their hooves are hardly touch-ing the ground.' He drank another sip and stepped up closer to the picture. 'Come here, come on.' Rolf got up and stood next to him. 'And now look at their back legs, the way the horse is pushing them backwards, with its ankles bent back. And you know what, that's what's wrong. When the front legs reach out so far and high without touching the ground,' he tapped the picture with his free hand, 'the back legs are already back to the centre of gravity, and that's here,' he tapped the horse's belly, 'well under the body. But Volkers couldn't see that back then. No human eye can make out the movement when they're galloping. This is the dream gallop phase, Rolf.'

They sat down again and drank. It was dark outside now, and Rolf saw their reflection in the windowpane. There were no curtains. 'I need your help, Horses Schäfer.' He picked up the bottle and divided what was left between their glasses.

'There is no Horses Schäfer any more, Rolf.' Schäfer looked at him and smiled. 'I haven't been to the track for years now. That's what you mean, isn't it?'

'I gotta win. There's no other way. I have to win, Schäfer.'

'When you have to win you always lose.'

'But you, you won so often. You always used to tell me. Eight hundred, nine hundred, two thousand, six thousand. You always used to say the chance is there. You always used to say you understand horses better than . . .'

'Than people? Did I say that?' Schäfer looked at his full glass and the empty bottle; he was drinking more slowly now. 'Most of it's luck, Rolf, that's the whole secret. And a little bit of instinct. I used to know people who'd never bet and then they won a triple, twelve hundred to one, and not even with a combination.'

'You're telling me you were just lucky all those years?'

'No,' Schäfer laughed. 'Look around you.'

'What if I try it, if I try on my own, at least tell me what to do. I have to try it at least.'

'Buy yourself a paper. *Sportwelt*, that's got everything you'll need to know. Stats, form curve, does the horse know the jockey, and if you like a name, Sea Lilly or Yes I Will Win, then go for it. If you want to make big money, Rolf, then only go for triples. Pick three horses as a combination, then it doesn't matter what order they come home in. That'll cost you sixty if you play for ten. Always bet on the full odds. Make sure you have at least one long-shot on your list, otherwise you won't get good odds. Not all long-shots are losers. But don't take the ones with the highest odds, look at the outsiders whose form's on the up. And don't give up if you make a loss, keep telling yourself, I'll make the big money in the next race. As long as it wasn't the last race of the day.' He laughed again and took a sip from his glass. 'And only bet on the races with good odds. You want to go next Saturday, right?'

'Yeah,' said Rolf, 'I have to.'

'How much do you want to risk?'

'Three hundred and thirty. That's all I've got.'

'That's the same as I get, Rolf. Every month.' They looked at each other and nodded. Schäfer told him a couple of other things to watch out for when the horses were on show in the paddock, that horses that used to be good, 'you can tell from the stats, Rolf,' could suddenly turn around after a long dry stretch, 'and then they have damn good odds,' told him about the sensations he'd experienced, 'the great outsiders were suddenly great winners,' named a few jockeys and trainers for him to remember, said he should listen every now and then to the commentator's tips because he had insider knowledge, 'but if you have an instinct, if you're sure of yourself, don't let yourself be swayed.' But Rolf knew he had no real chance if Horses Schäfer didn't come along with him. And Schäfer downed his drink in one.

'Beginners, Rolf, beginners are often the luckiest, and that's all that counts.' Then they said goodbye, and as Rolf walked down the stairs he knew there was no going back now, but he had nothing to lose, only the month's money.

They wouldn't starve if he lost. He still had a couple of emergency notes tucked away between his videotapes. And if he won . . . It didn't have to be the whole three thousand at once; he could make a down-payment with the vet for twelve hundred, fourteen hundred. And as he walked home through the dark streets he imagined the horses galloping past him to the finishing post.

'The field's just coming in to the far turn. In the lead still Planet Pony, close behind him Poppy Flower, just being challenged by Dream Believer . . . Lonely Affair gaining ground. Now Miss Moneypenny's picking up on the inside . . . all the others in a close pack. Only Elvis's Love Song at the tail end of the field.' Voices and colours, people and horses. Look how many people bring their dogs to the racetrack.

Rolf walked through the night. He didn't know what time it was, he didn't know exactly where he was or how long he'd have to walk to get home. He was drunk, and he reeled slightly, stopped now and then and held himself up against a wall. You can tell the winner from the start. What a load of rubbish, he thought. He staggered on. 'This is the dream gallop phase,' he called into the dark, deserted street. The street seemed unfamiliar, as if it were in a different town. Although everything was going crazy in his head, he knew he was in his own town, but while he reeled towards the edge of town, to the east, he was somewhere else – voices, colours, people, horses.

'And they're heading for the final turn. Planet Pony two lengths in the lead ahead of Belonia, Poppy Flower's third,

Ahab gaining ground on the outside. Planet Pony in front of Belonia and Poppy Flower.'

The commentator's voice gets louder and louder. There's a ring. Piet barks. Schäfer is standing outside. He's wearing a brown jacket, sunglasses and a checked cap pulled low on his forehead. In one pocket of his jacket is a rolled-up newspaper. 'I thought you might be gone by now.'

'This is my dog, Piet.'

'Hello, Piet.'

'And you want to risk everything for him?' Schäfer asks, as they're standing at the cocktail booth drinking mojitos, and Rolf has told him everything.

'Yes,' says Rolf, 'I want him to live a long life.'

'For a dog,' says Schäfer, spreading out his paper. 'That'll bring you luck.' He's made all kinds of notes on the page with the second race, circled a couple of horses and written little numbers next to them. 'There's not much to win in the first race,' he says, 'but we'll raise our capital a little. It's a sure thing.' And he seems quite sure as he fills out the red-printed betting slip. 'We'll go for an exacta, number three to win and number five in second place. A bit risky but it'll come good, ninety percent. Gimme a hundred.'

'A hundred?'

'It'll only win us sixty or seventy in profit, max, if we bet a hundred. And we'll put that into the bets that are worth it.'

'One hundred.' Rolf gives him two notes. They walk past the paddock, surrounded by people leaning on the railing and watching the horses being led around by their reins by girls and young women. Schäfer stops. 'There, those are our boys.' They have numbers on their saddle cloths and Rolf sees their boys, two large brown horses with long legs, no riders yet. He's never looked at horses so closely before.

'Can't go wrong. Look how calmly and powerfully they're stepping. Number three's a winner. See his beautiful neck and shoulders? And number five'll come in second. I can feel it, Rolf, the others aren't much good, and our boys have two damn fine jockeys on board. Sure thing, Rolf.' They walk past all the people, a line of tables under canopies; they stand in the tight crowd there and fill out their betting slips. Rolf looks over to the grandstand on the other side of the track. He can make out the people, see the flash of binoculars. Schäfer is standing in line for one of the betting counters and waves the slip at him. And he's right, it is a sure thing.

'Number three, Winning Streak ahead of number five, Milliana and number seven, No Words, by a length and a head.' They win seventy euros, just like Horses Schäfer said.

And then it all goes so quickly, they drink another mojito, and the seventy euros are gone again, second race, a trifecta, Lady Diana screws it all up. 'Now we're back to zero,' says Schäfer, 'including the cocktails. Zero's my lucky number, you know. And we're on pretty good form. It's the form that counts, Rolf, like with the horses.'

'It's the form that counts,' Rolf called out into the deserted street, then sat down on a doorstep. He rifled through his pockets, found a cigarette and lit it. He hadn't smoked for years, just like Schäfer, who'd had two packs with him and smoked one after another. Rolf was just about to fall asleep, but then he leapt up suddenly, the night no longer still.

'Copper Rose coming up behind the leading trio, Copper Rose one head behind, challenging now, half a head, behind her Lonely Affair with Ahab picking up. And Shadow Queen coming into the picture now. At the rear still Elvis's Love Song. They're coming into the last turn.'

'Be right back,' says Schäfer. He puts his cocktail down and walks over to an old man standing right by the hedge on the edge of the track, who's waved to him a couple of times now. Rolf finishes his mojito, then takes Schäfer's. He drinks and closes his eyes. He hears and sees the starting gate leaping open again and the horses galloping off. 'No human eye can make out the movement when they gallop.' But it seems to him as if he can see the nine horses' front legs thrusting into the air almost in sync. And then they ran, disappeared from his view, galloped around the track, the fifth race, a hundred and twenty euros down, sixty euros in the pot, a trifecta, a triple combination, and he hears the commentator's voice again: 'Dancing Mo two lengths in the lead,' hears Schäfer's voice next to him again: 'Don't worry, he'll fall back, they'll get him,' and Horses Schäfer is right, he's only third on the final straight, 'Dancing Mo a short head in front of Tulipe, Tulipe neck-and-neck now, no changes at the front, Quadriga and Saxon Storm a length and a half ahead of Dancing Mo and Tulipe, Dancing Mo or Tulipe, Dancing Mo or Tulipe . . . looks like the photo will have to decide. Quadriga first before Saxon Storm, then Dancing Mo or Tulipe. This'll be interesting, the decision's just coming up, don't throw away your betting slips, ladies and gentlemen.' And he hears the voice of Horses Schäfer next to him again: 'We'll get it, we've got it,

Tulipe in third place, we're really gonna rake it in, your dog's gonna live for years and years.'

'Got a couple of damn good tips for the last race but one,' Schäfer whispers next to him, 'the old guy over there's an ex-jockey, used to win me a lot of money. Trust me, Rolf, we're gonna clean up now. And if the worst comes to the worst we've always got the last race, but we don't even need it, the guy's worth his weight in gold, and I've got two horses in the last race that no one's reckoning with. We're on damn good form, Rolf. Pretty close, you know, pretty close . . .' He lights up another. Rolf takes one too, reaching for the pack so hastily that a couple of cigarettes fall on the ground, and puts the pack in his pocket. 'Fill it out,' he says, 'fill it out,' and he gives Schäfer the money. Schäfer leans over the betting slip, Rolf drinks his mojito, then he walks to the men's room. He walks past all the people, hears them talking and laughing, sees them filling out their slips at the canopied tables that look like mangers, takes a quick look at the horses in the paddock and the grandstand on the other side of the track, walks past the long lines at the betting counters and feels like he's going to piss his pants any minute now, before he reaches the toilets. A man is standing by the sink, looking in the mirror. 'Copper Rose,' he whispers over and over, 'Copper Rose,' and his body sways to and fro.

'Oh no,' whispered Rolf, crossing the road, walking along the middle of the street, but the street was deserted, 'no Copper Rose for you, my friend.' He reeled back onto the sidewalk, and now he knew where he was. Ahead of him he saw the main street with all the kebab shops and bars. It had to be after twelve, and he looked at all the lights, people were hungry and thirsty at night too. He walked towards the lights, saw the red letters of 'Sports Bets' a couple of hundred yards ahead of him. He walked faster, almost running, he coughed, he felt like he was going to vomit, and his cough reverberated around the street almost like a slight echo. Then he was standing in front of the store window, looking at the picture of the galloping horse. A couple of men came out of the door, waving little slips of paper; not money, he could tell.

'Poppy Flower, Belonia and Lonely Affair coming up behind Planet Pony. Ahab and Shadow Queen closing in on the outside . . . Poppy Flower and Belonia . . . Poppy Flower on the inside, on the outside Belonia with Ahab and Shadow Queen . . . and Elvis's Love Song racing full-out by the rail . . . Elvis's Love Song making good ground now . . . there's no stopping Elvis's Love Song . . . Elvis's Love Song, followed by Poppy Flower and Shadow Queen . . . Shadow Queen's taking out Poppy Flower, Ahab pushing ahead of Poppy Flower, Shadow Queen leading Ahab and Poppy Flower now . . . Elvis's Love Song still in the lead . . . Elvis's Love Song takes the race, ahead of Shadow Queen and Ahab, Elvis's Love Song wins the City Utilities Prize, who'd have thought it, Elvis's Love Song followed by Shadow Queen and Ahab.'

They scream and hug each other, Rolf landing on the ground for a moment, but he jumps up again and throws his arms around Horses Schäfer and laughs and shouts. But Horses Schäfer is suddenly all calm and says: 'We've got it, Rolf, you've got it, let's wait for the payoffs, but I reckon we'll rake it in, Elvis and Shadow Queen and Captain Ahab made it, I told you they would. And Elvis was well back, but I told you, you can't tell the winner at the start.'

Rolf turned around, the red letters of 'Sports Bets' a good way behind him now. He dug into his pockets, so confused he didn't know where he'd put the money. For a good while as he staggered through the streets – he must have had a drink somewhere after the race – he'd thought he'd dreamt it all, 'this is the dream gallop phase,' had lost everything when he risked everything. But now he felt the big bundle of notes in the lining of his jacket. Four and a half thousand; Piet would live for years and years.

'How much d'you want, Schäfer?'

'It's yours, Rolf, for your dog. Gimme two hundred for the last race.'

And Rolf pictured Horses Schäfer winning a couple of thousand in the last race. And then he thought of Piet and walked on towards the edge of town, to the east where he lived, and he didn't see the three men walking behind him.

I'M STILL HERE!

There were three numbers that meant a whole lot in his life. Not everything – there were other things apart from boxing: his wife, their child – even though it wasn't born yet, not even in his wife's belly – a few good friends. But boxing was how he earned part of his living. The rest he earned between fights, sometimes as a removal man, sometimes on building sites, sometimes as a bouncer. Some of the clubs in Rotterdam wouldn't let black men work on the door, but he had a good reputation as a boxer.

His wife worked too, twelve hours every day in a pet food factory down by the harbour, but when they had their child, like they'd been dreaming of for years now – they were waiting until they had a bit more money – she'd have to stop working there. He wanted to do less boxing then, less travelling; he didn't want his child to see his freshly mashed-up face after the fights. A couple of people had offered him a chance to come in on a small boxing club, if he put a bit of money into it. He had a pretty good reputation as a boxer, despite the three numbers.

18 – 32 – 3. Eighteen victories, thirty-two defeats, three draws. He was what they called a 'journeyman' – they brought him in so that he'd lose. It wasn't as if he lost on purpose; he did his best, at least most of the time, but they put him up against boxers who were simply better than him, faster, more talented and perhaps on the brink of a promising career in the ring. But right now they had to get more experience and perhaps later on they'd fight for a title just like he'd dreamed of too, years back. He'd boxed in a good few countries: Germany, England, Italy, France, Austria, Spain, Belgium. He'd won his last fight at home in Rotterdam, almost two years ago now. His eighteenth victory. He'd knocked out a red-headed Irishman with skin as white as snow. He still knew the man's three numbers off by heart: 2 – 5 – 0. Not an up-and-coming talent and pretty slow, and he'd got him in the fourth of six rounds. He was glad he'd been able to fight that Irishman; he'd wanted to win again at last, with his wife sat in the small hall, only half-full, at home in Rotterdam.

Ever since then only the middle number had got bigger and bigger.

26, 27, 28 . . . Germany, Italy, France . . . 29, 30, 31 . . . Copenhagen, Brussels, Madrid. He'd lost his last fight in Amsterdam, but just like in the fights before that he'd known he was going to lose. His opponent had once been the Dutch champion, one fight away from the European championship, but then he'd been badly knocked out and needed a few easy victories to get his confidence back. 'If you let him have a bit of a go at you,' the ex-champion's people had said to him before the fight, 'if you show him his punches really hurt . . . there'll be a bit extra in it for you. Show him he's really good, if you get what I mean . . .' And he'd got it.

Now he was in Germany and everything had been arranged, as usual.

He pressed the beer glass to his swollen cheekbone, catching sight of his face in the mirror behind the bar. Although it was pretty dark and a whole load of bottles blocked his view, he could see the welts and bruises. Sometimes white boxers envied him his dark skin; their faces were black and blue and green when they'd taken a beating. His top lip arched slightly towards his nose, where his opponent's lead fist had hit him over and over again. He drained his glass and pushed it across the bar. '*Noch eins*?' asked the woman behind the bar, and he saw her looking at his beaten-up face, and he gave a quiet laugh. A black Dutchman from Rotterdam with a mashed-up face in some bar in a town in the east of Germany. '*Ja*,' he said, '*noch eins.*'

He spoke a bit of German from his couple of fights in Germany. He'd had a contact man in Berlin, he used to get him a fight now and then, but he hardly got in touch now. The former Eastern Bloc had taken over the market. Tomato cans from the Czech Republic, Poland and Russia were cheaper than him and pushed the prices down; they were usually brought in two for the price of one. He was on his own. A discontinued model, he thought, an old timer but still in pretty good condition. He laughed, reached into his pocket and felt the notes he'd rolled up, and then he looked in the mirror behind the bar again. A couple more fights, one or two thousand, a couple more welts and bruises, and then he'd take all his savings and put them into the boxing club. He'd be in charge of training, a bit of sparring now and then, getting the lads ready for the fights. He looked in the mirror; his wife, his child, the boxing club; he saw himself standing in the ring, the big focus mitts on his hands, a lad ducking and diving in front of him, and whenever he called out 'left' or 'right' or 'left – right – left,' the boy punched the mitts with a whistle of expelled air.

'You had a good fight tonight.' He saw a man behind him in the mirror. He turned around. There was another guy standing behind the man, but only the first one was talking. '*Verstehst du*, good fight, very good!'

He nodded. '*Ja*,' he said, '*danke*.' The men grinned. They were pretty tall and at least two categories above him in weight, and the one talking to him had almost no nose left; probably down to the light as well though. 'Very good, Holland fighter, very good!' The men were still grinning, and he leaned his back against the bar and put one hand down next to his beer glass.

'You gave him a good seeing to,' said the man with the broken nose, switching to German. 'Raik's in hospital now, needs a check-up to make sure his head's all right. *Verstehst du*, Holland fighter?'

He did understand; not every word, but he'd understood. 'Sorry, say "good luck" to Raik. *Guter Boxer, guter Kämpfer*, very good.'

'Ja,' said the other man, the one who hadn't said anything yet. He didn't seem to speak English; the conversation stayed in German. 'Raik's a good boxer, he could make it to European Champion, Raik's champion material. We all believed in him, Holland fighter.'

The Holland fighter tried to smile and pointed at his burst top lip. 'Good left hook.'

'You lads want a drink?' The barmaid was standing behind him; he felt her voice against the back of his neck. 'No,' said the man with the broken nose, and the other one shook his head. 'I'll have another one,' said the Holland fighter, holding onto his empty glass when she wanted to take it away until she put a full glass down in front of him. 'Thanks.'

'You drinking to your victory, are you?' They'd come closer to him now, the man with the broken nose leaning on the bar beside him.

'Win, lose, doesn't matter. Next fight, I lose. Today, I win. Lucky today, Raik is a good man but I win.' He spoke very slowly to remember the right words in German, then he raised his glass. 'To Raik, to boxing!' He drank. He watched the two men as he drank.

'You're drinking to Raik, Holland fighter?' The taciturn one was talking now; broken nose took a couple of loud breaths. 'To our Raik, who you messed up?'

He put down his glass. *Kaputt gemacht.* He knew that word. *Kaputt.* How often had he lain kaput on the floor of the ring, how often had fast young talents beaten him across the ring, and he'd tried not to go down, had looked for a gap, had tried to counter their attacks, had hoped for that one punch to end the whole match. This time he'd found the gap and his punch had landed. Raik fell over, tipped over backwards as straight as a die, and his skull slammed against the wood. The referee didn't need to count – Raik was out, out cold, and he'd seen his legs twitching as if he still wanted to take that one step back so the right hook didn't reach him. He hadn't hit a good right for so long, he'd put his whole body into that punch, he'd felt it hit home right up to his shoulder. He'd gone backwards into his corner, wiping the blood from his lip with his glove, he'd seen the referee spreading both arms wide above Raik, and then he'd thought over and over, not quite believing it: I've won, I've won, I'm still here!

But no one had cheered, no one took his arms and raised them up, the sign of the victor. I've won, he thought, but the hall was quiet; the local boxer, the local hero had lost, 14 - 0 - 0 was kaput now, and even his corner men, provided by the organisers in return for a dock in his pay, silently avoided his eyes. Raik was carried out of the ring, ambulance men waiting down below with a stretcher.

'Right hand,' he said, clenching his fist, 'good right hand, Raik not careful.' He'd got up from the bar stool, pushing his left leg forward slightly. Now he was standing so that the bar stool was between him and the broken nose, with the other man diagonally opposite.

'What did he say about our Raik?' The taciturn one turned to his friend for help.

'That he didn't take care,' said the broken nose. 'He said Raik didn't take care. Right, Holland fighter?'

The Dutchman nodded and pointed to his nose. 'You

often in England? English boxers very hard, very good. English boxers good to nose, not careful, huh?' He looked at the broken nose and tried to smile. He'd fought in England twice, he'd been to Italy, had stood in the ring in Barcelona, had taken the ferry to Copenhagen to box there. And soon he'd come in on a boxing club, and the banknotes he felt against his leg through his trouser pocket would be another step in that direction.

The man with the broken nose pounded his fist against the bar stool, so hard that it tipped over. His mouth was open and the Dutchman saw that he was missing a few teeth. And the Dutchman saw that the punch at the barstool had been pretty powerful, but not all that fast. He'd seen the twitch in his shoulder before the punch came. He stayed standing quite calmly, one fist held loosely at hip level. He knew he couldn't evade every punch, one man in front of him, one man beside him, but he could take a few blows, he had a good chin.

'No fighting, lads,' said the barmaid behind them. 'No fighting, please.'

'Fight? Just because something gets knocked over, doesn't mean there's a fight.' The man with the broken nose bent down and picked up the bar stool, not letting the Dutchman out of his sight, and slowly stood it up again at the bar. 'Or are you looking for a fight?'

'No,' he said, lowering his fist.

'There you go.' The other man put a hand on his shoulder, and he instantly had his left hand on the man's arm and pushed it away. The man with the broken nose laughed. 'You're fast, Holland fighter, you've got fast hands. You black boxers are usually pretty fast. Hey, bring him another beer on me, and a shot of something too, he could do with one.'

The man with the broken nose turned to the barmaid, then he sat down on the bar stool, making him a head taller than the Dutchman, still standing there perfectly calmly with his left foot forwards.

'Money,' the man with the broken nose said now, rubbing his thumb and forefinger together right in front of the Dutchman's face, and then he started humming; it was meant to sound like that seventies song, 'Money, Money, Money...' The barmaid put a new beer and a schnapps down next to his half-full glass. He didn't turn to her; all he could see was her hands. Pale blue fingernails.

'Our Raik,' said the other man, 'he's in hospital now, won't be fighting for a long time, maybe never again. You're a clever lad, Holland fighter... You are a clever lad, aren't you?'

He didn't answer. He knew now it was going to be a hard night and he took a deep breath in and out again. In and out again. He felt his legs trembling; he'd fought eight long rounds.

'Raik'd be happy if you thought a little about him.' The Dutchman looked at the guy with the broken nose, who was rubbing his thumb and forefinger together again. 'You made good money tonight, didn't you?'

'Yes,' he said, 'the hard way, with my face.'

'Now you listen to me,' said broken nose, 'you, my Dutch friend, have put Raik on ice for a good long while. Who knows if he'll ever... Raik's got a wife and a little kid, they'd be really grateful for a little present.'

'No,' said the Dutchman. He picked up the schnapps glass, held it in his outstretched hand, tipped it and poured the liquid slowly on the floor at the man's feet. He felt the roll of money in his pocket, he thought of Rotterdam, his wife and the child they were going to have, thought of the boxing club he was going to come in on.

He slammed the schnapps glass down on the bar, grabbed the beer glass with his left hand and said, 'No.'

He was standing in the little room, right by the window; the curtains were closed. Behind him, he heard his wife in the bathroom; the door was open and he heard her using her make-up and cosmetics stuff, a clinking of small bottles, glass and plastic, running water.

She started humming to herself now and he closed his eyes for a moment. Then he moved the curtain aside slightly. There was a car outside the house. The window on the driver's side was wound down, an arm dangling out. 'Are they still there?' asked his wife, but it couldn't be his wife, she was speaking German, and the voice sounded nothing like hers either. 'Yes,' he said, pulling the curtain closed again.

'You can wait here till they've gone. But no cops – I don't want any trouble, *verstehst du?*'

'Yes,' he said. 'No cops.' He went over to the table and sat down. He wasn't in Rotterdam, only his wife was there, alone in their little flat.

He drank a swig of the whisky the barmaid had poured him.

'I've got a room upstairs,' she'd said to him down in the

bar. 'My shift's over in a minute. You can come up and wait until those bastards have gone.'

He drank the whisky, feeling himself getting gradually drunk. His neck hurt, his arms and shoulders ached, and he could feel the swelling beneath his right eye pressing against his eyeball. He was tired; he didn't want to fight any more. He drank another swig, saw the glass trembling, the ice cubes clinking quietly, and he put his other hand on his trouser pocket. Why hadn't the bastards tried to see to him in the bar? But they'd left when he'd shown them he was ready to use the heavy beer glass in his left hand. 'We'll be seeing you,' they'd said. Now he was sitting with her and waiting. He put the whisky glass down; he was so tired, his head drooped onto his chest; she was standing behind him. She said something but he couldn't concentrate properly any more, all he could understand was 'wait' and 'time' and 'bastards'. He was dizzy, he meant to hold onto the table but he knocked the whisky glass over, it was almost empty and it rolled across the table and then fell to the floor without breaking. 'Sorry,' he said, holding onto the table with one hand and turning round to her. She smiled. 'No problem,' she said. She squatted down and picked up the glass.

She held it in one hand, squatting down in front of him and looking up at him. She had short blonde hair, and now he saw she was freshly made up. Bright red lips, and he turned around and went to the window. As he went to pull the curtains aside she held onto his arm. He looked at her, and she said, 'I've never . . . never had a . . .' she thought for a moment. 'Black, I've never . . .' she thought again, 'never touched such

92

dark skin,' and then she laughed. She was still holding onto his arm. 'Soft,' she said. He looked at the curtains and then at her hand. He was tired, so tired. He'd cheated on his wife once, before a fight in Madrid, with a little black-haired Spanish woman; he'd spent the whole night in a hotel with her. The next night in the ring, he'd taken one punch after another, left, right, hooks, jabs, and he felt like he couldn't keep his cover up whenever his opponent went for him, a little black-haired Spanish man. Left, right, hooks, jabs. The audience had booed and whistled; he was known for giving all he had, for defending himself with everything he had, for countering, pummelling his opponent's body, for testing them, his opponents, getting everything out of them, giving them a challenge they could learn from, but that night he'd let the other man beat his head in. His wife had cried when he'd come home, his face swollen and smashed, a cut on his cheekbone. She'd stroked his face and he'd told her quietly about the boxing club he could come in on, if he put a bit of money into it. A few more fights, just a few more fights.

'Come over here,' she said. 'Lie down, have a rest. You can stay all night if you like.' He nodded, and she took him by the arm and led him to the sofa against the wall by the table. It was a pretty large sofa with a couple of cushions on it, and it looked huge in the small room. He lay down and then she was sitting next to him. Her hands were on his chest, he closed his eyes, felt her unbuttoning his jacket and taking it off. He meant to say something, wanted to say no, but she said, 'Shhhh,' as if she were calming a young child. He wanted to get up and leave, no matter if they were waiting for him outside, but he stayed lying there, he'd fought eight long rounds. He'd have a rest, get some sleep and maybe let her stroke him to sleep, that was all. He wasn't going to cheat on his wife again, not ever. She laid her chest on his and said, 'You can stay all night.' And that calmed him somehow, her breathing very even, and he thought about a lot of things and gradually fell asleep.

He leapt up. He leapt up so quickly that she stumbled aside. He was all there again. 'No,' he said, laying his hand on his trouser pocket. 'My money, bitch.' The roll of notes had moved – had he felt her hands? He hadn't imagined it, even though he was wiped out and drunk and might have been half asleep, but now he was all there again. He stroked his shirt smooth. 'Bastard,' she said as he picked up his jacket and went to the door. 'They'll wreck your face, they'll wreck your face even more, your ugly black face!' She laughed, loud and shrill, and he could still hear her laughing as he ran down the stairs.

He ran. He thought of all his running through Rotterdam's harbour, running and running to keep his form, thought of the ships and cranes disappearing and only the sea still there. He heard them behind him. They'd jumped out of the car; now he saw tower blocks on either side, tall and white, the night strangely bright. He had to get to the dark, he had to disappear into the dark to shake them off. He tried to breathe evenly, took deep breaths in and out again, in and out again. He turned around for a moment; they'd already fallen back slightly. A few minutes ago one of them had been so close behind him that he could hear him breathing. He'd fought eight long, hard rounds, but he had enough breath for at least twelve. Oh no, they weren't going to get him, he'd be taking his money back to Rotterdam, to his wife, to the boxing club, and he'd run along the harbour in the evenings to keep in shape, he'd run until only the sea was still there, and he'd laugh about them.

He turned into a narrow, dark street, the street lights almost all broken, and he ran close up to the buildings so they couldn't see him.

He ran past old derelict houses, and when he turned around again he saw the tall white tower blocks behind the houses; he didn't see the men chasing him any more but he kept on running, not slowing down.

There were people standing there, a tight group outside one of the houses in the light of a street lamp; it seemed like the only lamp in the narrow road still working. They called something out as he ran past them; he heard them laughing, bottles clinking, but he kept looking ahead; he saw the dark street and he ran until he suddenly choked and he had to stop, leaning against a house, then falling to his knees and vomiting. He puked until everything blurred before his eyes and he thought he heard the referee counting. One, two, three . . . By eight he was back on his feet, wiping the vomit from his mouth and his jacket. All silent behind him. No footsteps, no shouts. He walked on slowly, the street leading ahead of him into a wider, brighter one. There were the tower blocks again, and he was suddenly scared. He wanted to stay in the dark, narrow road until morning came.

His things were in a hotel at the station but he didn't know where the station was, didn't know where he was. He walked on slowly, no cars coming along the road. He saw the white tower blocks ahead; they seemed uninhabited, large empty rectangles. He'd grown up in an estate of tower blocks in Rotterdam, had spent most of his youth there, often fighting on the street before he'd started boxing, he'd trained every day so he wouldn't have to fight on the street any more. And he didn't like the thought that he might have to fight on the street again, here in this German town.

Later, in a taxi to the station, he couldn't remember what had happened and how and in what order. He kept saying all the way, 'I'm still here, you bastards, I'm still here.' He said it in Dutch, said it in German and laughed in the driver's face watching him in the rear-view mirror. He was still holding the banknote in his hand he'd used to wave. He'd wrenched the door open, leapt onto the back seat, and then they drove off. A bottle shattered on the road behind them. They shouted something but he couldn't understand it, didn't want to understand it either, they were behind him, they stayed in their part of town and he drove off.

At first he'd thought it was his friends from the bar again, that they'd spotted him again and caught up with him, but they'd had more hair on their heads than these ones, walking beside him on either side, him in the middle of the road so he had more space, and maybe a car would come after all, he walked down the middle of the road between the tall, white tower blocks, and they were on the pavements, forming a kind of cordon.

'Piss off out of here, nigger!'

'You stink!'

'Get back to the jungle!'

'Looking for trouble, are you?'

He knew they'd get him if he started running. There was no referee here to take him out of the fight for exhaustion. He walked very slowly, keeping his head lowered, flexing his shoulders under his jacket. Five or six on one side, five or six on the other. He looked straight ahead, only seeing them out of the corners of his eyes. He knew one of them had to start, had to step out onto the road to him, and then the others would come too, then the dance would begin. He had a pen in his jacket pocket and he'd use it. Eyes, necks, all the soft spots.

The taxi pulled up right outside the door of his hotel. It was almost light now. The street was empty. He handed the driver the banknote. He said, 'OK,' and made a hand gesture when the driver wanted to give him change. The driver nodded, '*Danke.*' He got out and watched the taxi until it disappeared. He put his head back, blinking at the ever-lightening sky. He wouldn't sleep; he'd pick up his bag and get on the first train to Berlin, from there to Cologne and then straight home. He smelt the vomit on his jacket. It hurt to breathe. His legs trembled, he could barely feel them and he swayed to and fro. But none of that bothered him. Nineteen – thirty-two – three.

ALL THE LIGHTS

It's the last night I've got but I don't tell her that, and we walk through the streets, and I look at all the lights and then at her. She's just as beautiful as back then, as if we were still fifteen or sixteen, no, she was thirteen, and somehow she still has a part of back then inside her, and I look at all the lights and talk about this and that.

She says something and I say, 'Yeah, that's right,' and then we're silent for a while and keep walking until she stops outside one of those posh bars with fancy cocktails and fancy people, and she says, 'Here.'

I go to open the door for her but she's quicker, and I walk inside ahead of her. I look over to the bar and across the half-dark room, and I feel her standing behind me, and I walk over to one of the small tables. We sit down. At the bar and at the other tables, women and men are sitting in the twilight drinking brightly-coloured cocktails or coffee out of big round cups with no handles. I take a brief look at her;

she's reading the menu and I watch her hand moving slowly across the paper. I look at her face, and her lips are moving very slowly too, lots of pretty cocktails with brightly coloured straws and little umbrellas and coffee in big round cups with no handles. She moves her lips and stares at the paper, and then she crumples it up and says, 'Why can't you just leave me alone, why don't you get it? I don't want anything to do with you,' and even though she's said it so often before I just nod and look at her. She takes the crumpled letter with her when she gets up – why doesn't she leave it behind? – and I watch her go until she's at the door and turns around again and gives me an angry look, with a slight crease from the top of her nose up to her forehead, and then she's gone.

There's a small beer in front of me, I don't know where it came from, and she says, 'Well then . . . Cheers,' and I nod and says, 'Cheers,' and we clink glasses.

We put our glasses down almost simultaneously. She's drinking a dark red cocktail, blood orange or something like that, and there's a stripe of the stuff above her top lip. I try not to look her in the eye for too long, running my finger across my mouth a couple of times. She smiles, takes a serviette and wipes the red stripe away. I take a sip of beer and look into my glass. I hear her drinking too, I hear her coughing, then only the music and the quiet buzz of conversation from the other tables.

I put my fingertips on my beer glass and stroke across the curve and the long, thin stalk it stands on. It's one of those small glasses we used to call 'tulips' back then, but I haven't heard that for a long time now.

'Have you been in town a lot the last few years?'

'No,' I say, without looking up.

'Only on business then.' She laughs, and I don't know why, and that scares me, and I ask, 'Why are you laughing?' and she laughs, and I look at her top front teeth, the two in the middle a tiny bit longer than the ones next to them, but only a tiny little bit, and I see her laughing and her teeth even though she's so far away, she's walking across the sports hall with the other girls, but all I see is her and I lean my forehead against the glass.

'I'm just imagining,' she says, still laughing, 'I can't imagine it, you know, you in a suit . . .'

I nod. 'I couldn't imagine it either, back then.'

She stops laughing. 'Sorry,' she says.

'No,' I say. 'Don't be.'

'No, I'm glad.' She leans forward, and her face is quite close to mine. 'Glad you're doing well. I sometimes thought, over the years . . .'

'What did you think, over the years?'

'Well, you know.' She leans even further forward, and I feel a tiny drop of her somewhere below my cheekbone. 'I was so mean to you, back then, and I'm sorry.'

'No,' I say. 'Don't be,' and I can still feel the little drop and I tilt my head and wipe it away with my shoulder.

'I,' she says, 'I . . .' She reaches for the dark red cocktail, takes out the straw and puts it on the table, then she drinks a couple of mouthfuls, holding onto the glass with two hands. 'Maybe . . . I guess I wasn't ready, back then.'

'Why – why are you saying that?' I down my beer in

one draft and slam the glass on the table. No, I've got everything under control and I put it down carefully on the coast-
er. 'After all these years . . .'

'I haven't . . . haven't seen you for so long,' she says,
'and now . . . and now, don't get me wrong . . .'

'No, no,' I say. 'I understand. I understood you back then
as well.' I put the empty glass to my mouth again, feeling the
tiny leftover of beer on my lip, and then I say, 'Sorry.'

'No,' she says, and the little table moves because she's
moving too. 'Don't be.'

We look at each other, I nod, she smiles, I turn around
and gesture for the waiter. The guy looks pretty gay in his
skin-tight lilac shirt, and I smile at him the way I want to
smile at her. 'Hey, faggot,' I say. 'Lonely, are you?' No, I just
think it and order a small beer. 'Do you want anything else?'
I ask her, and she shakes her head. The waiter takes my empty glass and scuttles off to the bar.

'And you really want to stay in town?' She rests her
chin on both hands, and I nod and try to smile and say,
'We'll see.'

'And your business?'

'Oh yeah,' I say. 'It's going . . . going pretty well. Can't
complain.'

'That's a nice hotel you're staying at.'

'Yes,' I say. 'It's not bad, it's really not . . . but in the long
term . . .'

'True,' she says. 'You could get a flat, I know someone . . .
I mean, if you want . . .'

'We'll see,' I say, and then my beer comes at last, and I

pick up the glass and drink and think about the hotel and the flat and her, about meeting her three days ago, even though she's sitting right in front of me, think about her teacup still standing in the room that's not mine, standing on the table for three days now. Rosehip tea. I don't know anyone else who drinks that kind of thing, and the teabag's still next to the cup, small, brown and shrivelled. I put the empty beer glass on the table and get up. 'Got to go to the little boy's room.' I walk around between the tables looking for the toilet, a woman and a man, at four or five little tables, all with a candle on them, just like ours, woman – woman – woman, two men alone at one table, with a candle as well, but nobody all on their own, the gay waiter standing behind the bar and flirting with a woman, and suddenly he doesn't look gay at all, and then I spot the toilet doors at last in an alcove beside the bar. A man on the left, a woman on the right, and I stumble into the door, and before I open it I turn around again. Our table is a long way off now; she's sitting with her back to me, resting her chin on both arms, and not moving.

I stand at the wash-basin, the cold water running out of my hair and over my face. I look in the mirror. I'm wearing a white shirt I bought this morning. I never usually wear white shirts or suits either, and now the water's dripping out of my hair and off my face onto the shirt, making tiny stains on the material. I see my pale face and try to smile and support myself on the edge of the basin.

'Am I on my own, you mean?' I nod. 'No wife, no children. Just . . . just business, you know . . .'

'And . . .'

'Do I ever think about it, you want to know? Yes, sometimes.' I look at the cup between us on the table in the hotel room. I ordered a whisky, I've been holding the glass in my right hand for ten minutes, and the three ice cubes are getting smaller and smaller. Rosehip tea. I don't know anyone who drinks that kind of thing, and then the cup's suddenly empty, and the teabag's on the table next to the cup, small, brown and shrivelled.

'Am I on my own?' I grin at the mirror and say, 'Not yet, but I soon will be,' and when the door opens and closes again and there's some guy behind me I turn around, grab him by the throat with my left hand, push him against the wall and press his head up against the tiles. 'Keep your hands off her, you bastard, you keep your fucking hands off her.'

He wants to say something but I'm holding him so tightly by the throat that only his lips move, and I put my right hand over his mouth and press his head even harder against the wall. 'Don't touch her.' I whisper in his ear. 'You keep your fucking hands off her.' He's quiet now, not moving, breathing in and out again very quickly, and I feel his breath on my hand. I let him go. I turn around and look at him in the mirror. He's pale and silent.

'Sorry,' I say. 'It's nothing to do with you, you bastard.'

I dry my face on a paper towel. I'm scared someone will come through the door – I want to be with her just a little bit longer. I open the door and see her far away at our table, pushing the candle to and fro, and I can tell she must be smiling. I go to the bar and pay our bill, and then I'm back with her. 'Let's get out of here,' I say, putting my hand on her shoulder very carefully. 'Let's go somewhere else. Please.' Her shoulder moves, and I take my hand away again.

'Are you not feeling well?' She gets up, and I take a few steps back.

'No, no, I'm fine.' I see someone going to the toilets, but it's a woman. 'I just need a bit of fresh air. Let's go somewhere else. Pool – can you play pool?'

'A little bit,' she says, and then we walk past all the tables and candles and go outside.

The night's almost over, and we're walking through the streets, and I look at all the lights and then at her, but mostly at the lights. She's just as beautiful as back then, as if we were still fifteen or sixteen . . . and somehow she still has a part of back then inside her, and we walk through the empty streets and stop in front of shop windows and talk about this and that.

'You played well just then,' I say.

'Oh no,' she laughs, 'only because you . . .'

'No, no,' I say. 'I wasn't on good form today, but you . . . you had a bit of luck, but you were really good.' She leans over the table and I'm standing behind her, I take her arm and say, 'Just a little bit, a tiny bit further to the left. You have to hit it on the arse.'

'On the arse?' She's leaning over the table, one eye pressed closed, moving the cue to and fro. 'Further to the side,' I say, shifting her arm very carefully. She looks up at me, one eye still pressed closed, with a crease from the top of her nose up to her forehead. She pots the ball, and I shoot mine off the cushions and across the table but don't pot them, let them stop before the pockets, because I want to see her happy when she wins.

We're standing in front of a shop window with all sorts of shoes on display, a tiny pair right at the front. I look at my watch. In eight hours, I'll be picking up my bags and disappearing. 'It's late,' she says.

'It's late,' I say and look at the tiny pair of shoes and walk on slowly. I haven't smoked all evening and I take out my pack and light one up. I turn around, she's still standing in the light of the shop window, and I take a drag at my cigarette, then I flick it against the wall. A few small sparks fall onto the pavement with the cigarette. She comes towards me slowly. 'I'll walk you home,' I say. 'Then I have to go to the hotel.'

'Do you know where I live now?' I nod. 'How come . . . ?'

'Someone told me.' We keep walking. It's not far to her flat, and I walk very slowly and stop at every shop window, even the ones only displaying ring binders.

'If you really stay here . . . '

'I'm sure it'll work out,' I say, standing in front of a shop; nothing to see in this one, just the counter at the back of the room, long and dark.

'There are plenty of flats free round my way, if you like, I know someone . . . '

'Let's . . . let's not talk about it now.' I look into the shop, then we walk on, the road empty, just a couple of cars driving past now and then, and I see the lights of the cars and the lights of the lamps on the edge of the street, and then we're standing outside her house. I light up a cigarette. 'You smoke?'

'Sometimes,' I say.

'Have you got one for me?' I want to give her mine, I'm holding it away from me between my thumb and forefinger with the lit tip downwards, but then I push it back between my lips and hold the box out to her. She takes one out and I give her a light.

'I used to smoke too,' she says, 'a while ago now, though.'

She smokes hastily and quickly, and blows the smoke away to one side. 'When . . .'

'Soon,' I say. 'Maybe tomorrow even, I have to sort out a couple of things, work and the hotel and that.'

'I . . . I'm so glad we met up again, that you're . . .'

'Yes,' I say, and I want to lean in to her but then I see the taxi driving slowly down the road, the sign on the roof glowing yellow.

I raise my arm and wave, twice, three times, and it comes over slowly and halts. The window's wound down, and I say, 'I'll just be a minute.'

I throw away my cigarette, lean up close to her and say, 'Look after yourself,' and I lay my hand on her hair for just a moment. She doesn't say anything, and I turn away and walk over to the taxi. At first I want to sit in the front, but then I get into the back. 'The station,' I say. That's where my bag is, in a locker. I'll sit down on a bench and wait for the morning and the train.

RIDING THE RAILS

All the nights on trains. That's what I still think of, often. Sometimes, in my dreams, I'm back on the trains again, riding the rails from town to town with Blondie. Outside, all the lights, us drinking beer or whisky, usually in silence, rarely making plans, counting up our money.

The conductor looks tired; there's a man asleep on his seat, his mouth gaping. Blondie looks at me and says, 'When the time comes . . . when I've got them . . . don't ever leave me alone too long with those bastards.'

'Sure,' I say. 'I'll always look after you.' We were passing through some small town or other. We looked out at the lights in silence.

I met him out in Torgau. He was doing time for something petty, a bit of theft, bit of drugs, that kind of thing.

He was queer, I could tell straight away, not that I usually had an eye for his type. I'd often sat in bars and pubs in strange towns and wondered why there wasn't a single woman in there, and sometimes one of the guys had bought me a beer, and when I caught on the whole thing sometimes ended down at the police station – but not always, and that wasn't why I was in Torgau.

I can't remember how I noticed, and I don't know where exactly it was that I first saw him. Probably in the corridor but maybe in the yard or the gym. It can't have been the way he walked, he walked pretty normally actually, not swaying his arse or anything. It was something about his face, about the way he looked at you. It wasn't that he looked like a woman or acted all girly; he came across as very young, almost like a child, even though he was maybe in his mid, late twenties, and he had this smile . . . I think if you looked at his smile for too long you got scared, especially where we were, that you'd have to go to him, hug him or something.

I'd met a good few queers in the three jails I'd been in. I'd seen prison gays who couldn't hold out all the years but only loved women outside. Prison-marriages, lags who'd shared a cell for years and quarrelled about nothing all day long like old grey couples but forgot about it all every night. I'd seen guys get beaten up for looking at someone 'queer'; usually they hadn't done anything at all. But in all the years I'd never made friends with any of them. I'd made sure I never spent too much time with them – no good for your reputation.

It was strange. I saw him and I knew right away that he'd never go to bed with a woman, not a chance. Later on he told me it had happened a couple of times actually, on drugs, and that he'd felt so cold every time that he'd had to get up and leave right in the middle.

His hair. I always remember his hair: blond, shiny and pale at his temples; it looked almost like he was starting to go white there. Someone grabbed him by the hair; that was the first time I stood directly in front of him. He had quite long hair, flopping over his forehead. 'Let him go,' I said. He peered at me through one eye; the guy's arm was covering his other eye, the guy holding him by the hair. 'You keep out of it, it's none of your fucking business.'

And the guy was right, it was none of my fucking business, but once I'd stopped and said 'Let him go' – even though I didn't know what it was all about, even though I knew the queer wasn't clean and needed to powder his nose now and then and that kind of thing always made for trouble sooner or later – I'd held out my hand to him and I couldn't just take it back again, not any more. A couple of weeks beforehand my cellmate had tried to kill himself, wanted to top himself. 'Let him go.'

I knew the guy wouldn't let him go. I could have tried persuading him for hours, maybe then a snout might have come along and the guy would have acted like he was putting his arm round Blondie, like they were the best of friends having a wee chat in the corridor. And then it all went very fast, the guy was on the floor and Blondie said 'Ouch,' and put his hands on his head, and I saw that the guy was gripping a few hairs between his fingers, rolling to the wall, his arm splayed away from his body. I'd caught him unawares.

I shoved Blondie away from him, pushed him along the

corridor, a couple of guys standing by their doors watching us, and I said, 'Go on, piss off back to your cell.'

He nodded, still holding his head as he walked down the corridor. He hadn't said thanks or anything, he'd just nodded and left, but when he'd peered at me through one eye, the guy's arm across his face, there'd been something in his eye . . . In bed that evening I thought a lot about it, there was something there, as if he'd known at that moment that we'd be riding the rails, later on.

'You a gay-lover, are you?' I'd known it'd happen and it'd stay that way, for the rest of my time. 'Gay-lover, eh? You doing her, are you?' I hit out, pummelled into the guys, tried to beat the shit out of them before they beat it out of me. I felt time passing more and more slowly. Six months to go.

The guy I'd knocked down had a couple of business ventures going, and he gave me everything back. I'd known that too when I'd said 'Let him go,' because by that point I'd already punched him. And when he went down, Blondie's hair between his fingers, I could already feel the fists on my back, my belly and my face.

'Sorry,' said Blondie.

'Forget it.' His name was Stephan. He was half-Polish but you couldn't tell from looking. Now and then we stood side by side in the yard and he smoked a cigarette, although he didn't usually.

'Have you got a wife outside, I mean, is there a girl waiting for you?'

'No,' I said, 'but don't get your hopes up, little brother.'

He grinned; no, he smiled. 'You're not my type anyway.'

'What happened there?' I pointed at his eye, almost touching his face with my finger, then withdrew it again. His eye was blue and green, swollen half-shut.

'And you?' I raised my swollen top lip and whistled through the new gap in my teeth. 'I asked you, gayboy,' I said, whistling two or three off notes.

'Walked into a door,' he said, still smiling.

'Yeah,' I said, 'easily done, too many doors round here.'

He got out two months before me. We didn't say good-bye. He'd told me once he'd be going to Halle. I was there now and then myself, and I kind of knew I'd see him again, that the story wasn't over yet, hadn't even really begun, in the corridor in Torgau where Blondie had lost a few hairs.

'Your pussy gone now, is she? Bet you're sad now with no one to fuck, huh?'

I didn't hit out any more, didn't pummel into the guys, didn't try to beat the shit out of them any more. I just walked past them, walked down the corridors and round the yard on my own and felt time passing more and more slowly.

My sister had never written to me but I knew she was living in Köthen, that she had a kid with some guy who worked in some bar in Köthen.

My sister sat on the edge of the sandpit, next to her brightly-coloured sand moulds and little plastic spades, and in front of her the kid sat in the sand, digging a hole and putting the sand in a blue bucket. I stood between the trees and looked over at them. I didn't know how long I'd been standing there, it was nearly evening. I didn't even know if the kid was a boy or a girl. It had blond hair and a small round face with a large nose. But I was a long way off so maybe the nose wasn't all that large, and maybe all little kids had large noses. Two, two and a half; I tried to work out how old it was, but then I gave up and walked back between the trees to the station. I had a room above a bar there, maybe it was even the bar where the kid's father worked, I had no idea, I'd been away too long, but I didn't really care anyway.

'How's it going?'

'Fine, thanks. Nice of you to come by. It's been a long time. This is your uncle.' She picked up the kid and handed it to me. 'Hello,' I said, stroking the blond hair cautiously. Sometimes I imagined her making coffee and serving cake, some kind of cake, and then I started wondering what sort of cake it might be and if she might have made it herself and how many teeth little kids are supposed to have before they can eat cake, with apples or cherries on top, but with the stones taken out . . . I sat in my room and knew I'd leave again without visiting her, maybe back to Leipzig, maybe to Halle . . . The window was open and I looked outside, even though it was dark by now and all that was opposite was a derelict house.

There was a club not far from the station. I could hear the music at night, I could hear the trains as well, sometimes I heard women's voices, or were they still girls? They were down on the street, probably going to the club. It must have been a pretty big place; I heard cars coming and driving off. I hadn't been to a club for years now.

I stood at the bar, watching the dance floor. It was pretty full, Friday night. Most of the people here looked pretty young: eighteen, nineteen, early twenties. Two young women stood next to me at the bar, drinking white wine. They'd looked over at me a couple of times but I didn't know what to do. I watched the people dancing and sipped at my beer.

I'd been with a woman I used to know in Leipzig for a couple of days. Actually I'd gone to visit her husband but she was divorced now and alone, and it hadn't worked out. I'd been away too long and I'd forgotten everything, even though I'd dreamed almost every night of not being alone when I got out.

'It'll be all right,' she said. 'It'll sort itself out,' and she was probably right, but when we lay together and she stroked me and I stroked her the fear and the cold didn't go away, and I left while she was asleep.

I drank shots with my beer, and after four shots I noticed I needed to dance. The music was pretty good, sounded like George Michael, I'd liked him as a kid, but I'd even have danced to Beethoven. I wanted to move in among the dancers, shut my eyes and feel them, feel them close and hear only the music. I downed another shot. The girls next to me had disappeared, and I went over to the dance floor, wanting to disappear too, closed my eyes and started moving slowly. I was a bit scared I might have forgotten how to do that as well, but once I moved my feet to the rhythm my shoulders started relaxing, my arms still dangling on either side, but then I raised them slightly, moving them at chest level. Someone nudged me in the back, pretty hard, but it didn't bother me, I was dancing and forgetting everything, not thinking of Blondie and the long corridors any more, not thinking of my sister living a few streets away with her kid and her man, and at that moment, in among all the people touching me and nudging me now and then, at that moment I thought there must be something like happiness, somewhere out there, and the fear and the cold I'd been dragging around with me since I'd got out were gone. I'd never have thought our trip would start here, but maybe, probably, it had already begun long before that, inside, on the corridor, when he'd lost a bushel of hair.

The girl was pretty far gone but so was I. We'd been dancing together, or not really together, just facing each other, but on some songs we held hands and looked at each other, our faces up close. I saw she had on a pretty thick layer of make up, with sweat running down over it. And she smelled strongly of alcohol, something sickly-sweet, but that didn't bother me when she suddenly leant towards me and leaned her forehead against mine and I had to kiss her. We danced. We danced for a long time, we danced until we sweated and the sweat ran down our faces, and then we staggered to the exit.

'What are you doing here, Stephan?' I asked, holding onto the girl as she tried to drag me on towards the exit and then clung onto me.

'Pretty little girlfriend,' he said. A few minutes back, when we could hardly dance any more and I'd laid my head on the girl's shoulder, I'd had a feeling I'd seen his blond hair somewhere in the crowd. But there were plenty of blond guys out there and he'd never told me he did business in Köthen. And he was doing business, I could tell straight away, even though the girl was tugging at me and wanting to leave and I had to concentrate to stop Blondie from swaying and whirling. Some guy palmed him a note, and he pressed something into his hand. The guy clenched his fist, opened it again for a moment and looked at his hand, then grinned, turned away and headed for the toilets. 'It'll take a while,' Blondie called after him, 'but then you'll go mental.'

'What's all this crap?' I said, shoving him in the chest. The girl let go of me and stumbled against the wall. 'Let's go,' she said, turning her face to me. Her eyes opened and closed, but it was just the sweat running down her face.

'Just a minute,' I said. 'Just a bit. Wait a minute, sweetheart.' But she didn't want to be my sweetheart any more, and I watched her swaying to the exit, raising both hands and saying something I didn't understand.

'Don't you want to go after her?' Blondie put his hand on my shoulder.

'What are you doing in Köthen, Stephan? If they catch you here – Christ, you're not even being careful!' I took the note out of his other hand and shoved it into his jacket pocket.

'Don't worry, little brother,' he patted my shoulder a couple of times. 'They're all village idiots here, they've got no idea, they won't even notice.' He winked at me and smiled. There it was again, his smile; he looked as innocent as a child. You wanted to help him, even though he might not even need any help, like a child you couldn't help being fond of. Even if he'd done something really bad all he had to do was smile and you'd stroke his hair and everything would be all right again. I stumbled and held onto the wall where the girl had just been leaning. I looked towards the exit but she'd disappeared.

'And you know what the best bit is?' I closed my eyes, but he was right by my ear. 'Painkillers. You get it, painkillers. I'm ripping these village idiots off and they don't even notice!' He laughed, and then I heard him rummaging in his pockets. 'No one knows the brand; they're from Poland with this little star on them. Like a pill, like ecstasy.' I opened my eyes and saw the little white pill right in front of me, saw the star in the middle as well, and then there were two guys, they gave him two notes, and he gave them the pill and got another pill out of a little bag that he put back in his jacket pocket afterwards. 'And be careful, lads, they're . . .' But they were gone. I gave myself a shake and tried to clear my head. I'd need a clear head soon enough, I was sure of that.

'How long have you been standing here now?'

'For a while, quite a while, I've earned a packet, hey, I'll get you a drink!' He held the notes in front of my nose, but I batted his hand away.

'Right, come on, we're getting out of here!' I dragged him to the exit, and it was about time because they were coming for him now, a couple of yards behind us, the first of the village idiots who'd noticed that the pills Blondie was selling didn't make them go quite as mental as he'd promised. And even though they weren't in any pain, they still wanted their money back and they wanted to inflict some pain on Blondie. Five or six guys, young lads waving their arms and pointing at us, or only at him but I'd decided – no, not decided, it had just happened, and I was with him, right in the thick of it, and I let it happen. 'Come on, let's go!' Then we were outside, and they were still coming after us, five or six young lads, and there were more and more of them now. We walked towards the station, and then we ran, and I shouted, 'You fucking idiot – painkillers!' And he laughed as we ran, and suddenly I couldn't help laughing either, and I got a stitch.

'Painkillers, you halfwits bought Polish painkillers!'

Did he shout, did I shout? Did we both shout while the village idiots were coming after us? We laughed and ran.

He lay next to me in bed and I watched him sleeping. We were in a cheap dive and the bed was far too small for two. We'd stayed in good hotels a couple of times, separate beds, and one time we'd had a room each. But when I'd woken up early he was lying on the carpet next to my bed. He had a talent for opening doors, and I'd found a blanket and covered him over.

He looked pretty pale lying next to me in bed, asleep, his head shifting on the pillow now and then. He'd snorted something to help him sleep, probably heroin. He always made sure I didn't watch him doing it, even though I'd never said anything, and I needed some of it myself some nights. We took trains from town to town, usually medium-sized towns, sometimes the big cities, Cologne, Hamburg, Berlin, he'd been almost everywhere and he knew where we could go on tour. I can't remember exactly where we'd started it all, it was probably some kind of coincidence, happened without us thinking much about it, turned out that way while we were riding the rails and didn't know where to go next. Sometimes I thought . . . No, I hardly ever thought about it, it was as if we belonged together, like brothers, I told myself, and when we were sitting on trains, sleeping in hotel rooms, walking through the towns, it was as if we had to keep moving, and everything else that was behind us, that lay before us, was strangely blurred. We didn't care about it, we were riding the rails.

I saw them sometimes when I slept. They were usually older men, sometimes young ones too. I saw the fear on their faces, in their eyes. Usually I didn't even have to touch them. One old man had started crying. He was wearing a bit of make up, blusher on his cheeks – a painted old man crying and turning to the wall while I went though his pockets.

'Stop crying, you queen,' said Blondie, and before I could stop him he slapped him across the face. 'Leave it out,' I said, but he just looked at his hand, stained with blusher and the old man's tears. 'Dirty bastard, you fucking dirty bastard!' He wiped his hand clean on the old man's jacket. 'This fucking queen's got me all dirty.'

'Leave it,' I said, taking a couple of notes out of the old man's wallet. He was still crying and he'd started trembling. I put the wallet back in his jacket and the old man trembled and said, 'Please don't hurt me.' That had been up on the coast, by the door to the basement in a house near where the rent boys stood at night.

'You mustn't ever leave me alone then,' said Blondie. He'd woken up. His eyes were blue, dark blue. Up on the coast, we'd often stood by the sea together.

'How d'you mean?' I asked, turning my head to look at the ceiling. The light was on, a couple of flies perched around it.

'When I go with them,' he said, and I felt him moving his legs, 'promise me you'll never . . .'

'Sure,' I said. 'You know that, Stephan, you know I'll be there then, you know I'll always come. We're raking it in, you and me, they're all village idiots, even in Hamburg, even in Cologne, eh?' I laughed, and for a moment it looked like the light was flickering.

'Village idiots,' he said. He was talking pretty quietly now. I could hardly understand him and I turned back to him. 'We're doing pretty good,' he whispered.

'Yeah, we are,' I said, putting my hand down on the pillow next to him.

'Better than back then,' he whispered. 'Better than . . .'

'Yes,' I said, 'better than back then.'

'Can you get me something please?'

'Sure,' I said, 'if you want.'

'No,' he whispered. 'A glass of water's fine.'

'Or a whisky, what about a wee dram, Stephan, help you sleep . . . '

'No thanks, a glass of water's fine.' We looked at each other and he smiled. I got up and went to the table with the bottles of water and whisky. I drank a slug of whisky out of the bottle and poured a glass of water for him. I looked over at him and had another drink and saw his eyes moving, looking at me now. 'You know,' he said, 'sometimes . . .'

'Yeah?' I said, screwing the cap back on the whisky bottle. He didn't answer, and I asked, 'Shall I turn the light off?' I took the glass of water over to the bed. He'd closed his eyes and I sat down on the edge of the bed. His forehead was soaked in sweat, and I raised my hand but just put it down on the pillow next to him. 'You know,' I said, 'sometimes . . .' I drank his water and pushed the empty glass under the bed.

I saw their faces sometimes when I slept. There was one man who put up a bit of a fight. He was already near-naked and Blondie had taken his shirt off as well. Pretty young lad he was, with glasses, maybe a student. He was pretty well-built too but he wore glasses with black frames and pretty thick lenses. I didn't usually even have to touch them, but this young lad was in his room, his own little room, and he wanted to defend it, it wasn't just some cheap hotel, some corridor, some dark corner where he'd got himself a quick blow job, it was his own little home that he'd taken Stephan back to, and I'd almost come too late because the door was closed. Blondie hadn't managed to open the door for me. He'd been lying on the bed, the student on top of him, he was a pretty broad well-built lad, probably not a student at all, a queer builder or an office worker who lifted weights, and all I saw was Stephan's arms on the sheet next to the guy. 'You can tell the cops your story, eh, about picking up a rent boy. You hit him, eh? Did you force him?' There was a bottle of whisky on the bedside table; I unscrewed the cap. 'Maybe I'll go to the cops and tell them you beat him up.' I held his ID card in my hand and said, 'I bet your parents are nice people, eh?'

'I didn't hit anyone,' he said. His glasses were on the bedside table next to the bottle; one of the arms was broken. I drank a glug of the whisky and said something about compensation and was surprised he didn't start crying like the old man had cried, outside the basement door up on the coast. He pressed a hand to his eye but there was no blood, and with the other eye he looked between me and Stephan, who was sitting at the table buttoning up his shirt. I said, 'Stephan,' and I threw him the whisky bottle, but he didn't catch it and it fell on the floor and smashed. Was that the first time we went on tour?

I heard him breathing next to me and looked at the ceiling. The flies had gone.

We were sitting at a small table right by the huge window. It was night, and all the lights of the city lay twenty-seven floors below us. I don't know whose idea it had been to come to Leipzig. We'd passed through a couple of villages around it, knocking off a load of dodgy pills. Then we'd picked up two guys in a dark park next to the ethnology museum, and now we were high above the city, five-star hotel, drinking kir royale and champagne and looking out across the lights on all the buildings, in the streets, eating starters and desserts, cod liver and prunes in bacon, cheese platters and turkey medallions, waving over the waiters who came trundling between the tables with little carts. 'Would the gentlemen care for a choice pear brandy from the private distillery . . . ?'

'The gentlemen would,' said Stephan, and the waiter fussed around, placing two little glasses on the table and filling them up with even more fuss.

'Enjoy your drinks, gentlemen,' he said with a slight bow of his torso, then trundled off with his cart.

'Enjoy your drink, gentleman,' I said as I raised my glass.

'I will,' said Stephan, and then we touched glasses. We downed the choice pear brandy from some private distillery in one. 'What d'you reckon it costs?'

'No idea,' I said.

He nodded and tapped his breast pocket. 'I've got it covered.'

'And if not?'

'Then you'll have to box us out of here,' he said, patting my hand for a moment. 'When we're on tour together, you know, I'm never scared.' He patted my hand again, and when I went to take it away again he held onto it, and first I pulled a bit and then my arm went suddenly slack, and he lifted up my hand. 'Your hands are so small though,' he said, 'almost smaller than mine, see?' He was still holding onto my hand and now he put his other hand up against it. 'Doesn't it hurt when you punch them?' I leant back with a jerk, wrenching my arm away so that his hands fell on the table. He was sitting bent over the table, and for a tiny moment it looked as though he was going to lay his face on his hands. He still had a trace of lipstick on, although he'd wiped his lips with a tissue. He'd used black mascara on his lashes and eyebrows. We'd taken the money straight to the restaurant. 'A table for two!' And the waiters had given us a funny look, 'right by the window, if possible!' And the people at the other tables had turned around, maybe because I'd turned my sleeve up a bit and they could see the lizard. I took the champagne out of the cooler and filled our glasses. He drank a sip and said, 'You know, I've never drunk champagne before.' He'd leaned back as well; his face was in the shade now, not looking so pale any more. He smiled.

'I don't believe you.'

'Why not?' He drank another sip, then he took a piece of bread from the basket full of all different, probably exquisite slices of bread from some private bakery. 'You reckon just because I'm queer I ought to know all about champagne and that?'

'No,' I said, 'you know I didn't mean it like that, you know I . . .' I picked up my champagne and tried to down it in one, but the stuff fizzed so hard in my nose that I put it back down on the table halfway through.

'Yes,' he said, 'I know. I didn't mean it like that.' He dipped the piece of bread in the remains of his cod-liver paté. 'We're friends, aren't we, we're almost like . . .' He ate the bread and cod-liver paté and I picked up my glass. 'Yes,' I said, 'we are.' We drank and looked out at the city again. There seemed to be more and more lights down there, red lights and yellow and white, lights that flickered, lights that moved around and disappeared again. We were silent for a long while until one of the waiters came trundling up again with his cart. 'Would you care for a cigar, gentlemen?'

'You choose two for us,' I told him. 'Two good ones.'

Stephan nudged my leg under the table. 'We fancy a really good cigar, don't we Stephan?'

And then we smoked and the waiter trundled off with his cart. It had taken him ages to choose two cigars, present them to us and then prepare them. We smoked, smoked hectically and quickly, I hadn't smoked a cigar for years, and Stephan can't have done either, and the smoke hung between us in dense swathes.

'Do you think they're looking for us?'

'No,' I said, 'don't you worry, Stephan. Those guys would never go to the cops.'

'Even if they do,' he sucked at his cigar and thought for a moment, 'it doesn't make any difference.' He smiled, breathing out smoke.

'No,' I said, 'it doesn't make any difference.'

'Remember back in Torgau . . .'

'Not now,' I said, and he said, 'Sorry.'

'It's all right. Do you want a dessert?'

'Sure, why not?'

Looking out of the window, I could see the big bridge. A couple of ships in front of it, but it was almost dark. I was drinking whisky, my watch next to my glass.

'He's a pretty dodgy guy,' Stephan had said. 'Does all sorts of stuff. Sex toys and bondage and that. Picks up boys on the street, he's into picking them up off the street. I know where, and I know how. It's worth it, he's loaded.'

'How d'you know about him?'

'From a friend.'

'You're not as young as you used to be, Stephan.'

'Hey, come on.' He'd smiled, and then he'd added, 'Young enough for him, as long as I play along.'

'Play along?'

'You know, everything he wants. Even if it hurts.'

'If it hurts,' I'd said, and he'd kept on smiling.

'And your friend?'

'That lad in Berlin, you remember . . .'

'Yeah.' He'd been there for a while, while I'd been working in a bar with an old mate I knew from inside, serving customers, keeping the peace and whatever came up.

'I need a holiday,' he'd said.

'Sure, you take a bit of a rest.' He'd been there a couple of weeks, with his 'lad', while I was in the bar every night and couldn't sleep in the day, a bed in the back room, far too small for two, and I'd left the light on, but now we were riding the rails again.

'Come by around ten. His flat's out by the harbour, I'll write the address down for you.'

'No, I want to see it before. It's safer that way. Then I'll stay close by.'

And I was close by. I was drinking whisky and looking at the big bridge and the ships disappearing slowly in the darkness. There was one very large ship, with several decks one above the other. I ordered another whisky, then another. I looked at the hands of my watch.

There was a woman next to me at the bar, drinking as well, a large cocktail. I'd ordered it for her. 'Are you waiting for someone?' asked the woman. She'd asked me a couple of things before but I'd just answered yes or no and then ordered her the cocktail. It had been a long time since a woman had asked me to get her a drink.

'No,' I said, looking at the hands of my watch. Still time; Stephan would probably be going over to where the guy picked up his boys right now. His 'lad' in Berlin had told him everything. 'What if he doesn't come?' I'd asked. 'What if he takes someone else home?'

'You know me,' he'd said, 'I'm irresistible.'

'I've never seen you here before,' said the woman. 'You're not from round here, are you?'

'No,' I said, 'I'm not from round here.'

She drank her cocktail, stroking the end of her straw across her lips. 'Are you here on holiday or are you working?' She didn't stop chatting, and I picked up my glass and turned to face her. It was dark outside now, and it was pretty gloomy in the bar too, little candles burning on the tables even though most of them were empty. She wasn't that good looking, jaded, the corners of her mouth drooped, bags under her eyes, but her blonde hair shone in the light of the red lamp above the bar and she was nicely dressed, and the way she was dressed I could tell her body was still in pretty good shape, although it could all be playing tricks on me, the light and the whisky and the night. 'What about you,' I said, 'what do you get up to?'

She stroked her straw across her lips before she drank. 'This and that,' she said, pushing the glass aside and taking out the straw and holding it between two fingers and tapping it on the bar a couple of times. I nodded and looked past her at the big window, behind it the night. I nodded again and looked at her, and now she smiled and blushed and lowered her head a touch and looked at the bar.

Sometimes I think that was what it was, that smile, that blush, that lowered head, sometimes I think . . . A cheap tart, I'd thought in the bar when she sat down next to me, and she probably was one, maybe a professional, I'd thought, and maybe she was one, semi-professional, now and then, but that blush – no, it wasn't the smile so much, it was the blush, the lowered head, because just before she'd been asking stupid questions and laughing loudly. Sometimes I think she just did that for me at that moment, just acting because she could tell I'd like it. Sometimes I think, and sometimes I know, that all she did was give a stupid grin, that moment next to me, her head leaning forward into the red light of the lamp above the bar.

'Hey,' she said, 'you're a nice boy.'

'You're a nice girl,' I said. I looked at my watch and put it in my pocket.

I ran down the corridor. I wanted to get out of there. There was a man lying on the floor, one arm splayed strangely away from his body. 'Stephan,' I called out, but I knew he wasn't there. I'd searched the flat but all I'd found was sex toys. And special furniture, benches, stools. I found stuff only doctors have. I stood in the hallway, but there was no man on the floor any more. The door was open. I ran down the stairs. There'd been a couple of bushels of Blondie's hair on one of the pieces of furniture.

I ran down the street. I turned around and looked back at the house where Blondie had been just a couple of hours before. A taxi came, the sign on its roof glowing yellow. I waved and it stopped next to me. I opened the door and got in the back. 'To the station,' I said, and we were on our way.

THE SHORT HAPPY LIFE OF JOHANNES VETTERMANN

The man has a dog's head. An Alsatian, large ears protruding from his head, pointing towards the ceiling. The man with the dog's head is directly in the light of the large chandelier. Johannes Vettermann is lying on the floor, crawling backwards away from the man with the dog's head. But the man with the dog's head doesn't seem to be taking the slightest interest in him. He's holding a small, dark puppy in both hands, human hands, pressing it between the lapels of his jacket.

Now he opens his muzzle, a long pink tongue getting longer and longer until it touches the puppy's head. The dog-man is absolutely absorbed in licking the tiny head. Johannes Vettermann wonders whether he ought to pick up the ashtray from somewhere behind him on the bedside table, but the two of them look so placid there, the tiny dog looking him right in the eye. 'Father,' says the puppy all of a sudden, and Johannes Vettermann doesn't know if he means him or the dog-man. But the dog-man says it too, 'Father,' slurring slightly as he goes on licking. 'Father, father, father.' They won't stop, their muzzles hardly moving, as if they were ventriloquists.

And he's no longer crawling backwards, he's crawling towards the door again where there's a telephone on a table. There was a telephone on the bedside table but he smashed it against the wall because it kept ringing. No one knows he's here, but it kept ringing and ringing.

The table is a long way away, a large suite in the best hotel in town, five stars, twenty-seventh floor, and the way to the door is even longer now because he has to make a detour around the two dogs. 'Father, father, father.'

'Then you two can –' he whispers, 'then you two can help me out a bit, can't you?'

'Bad father, bad father!' Another man leaps at him from one side, Johannes Vettermann screaming out loud. The man is naked, tattooed all over his body, an eagle, a clown, faces, symbols, but that's not what scares Johannes Vettermann. It's the man's face, contorted into a terrifying grimace. He has no top lip, his bottom lip sags lopsidedly, dark red and swollen, while two jagged teeth point towards his nose like two thin, white fingers. And his eyes . . . The eyes stare at Johannes Vettermann with such rage that he tries to crawl under the king-size bed. He's still screaming. He squeezes his eyes shut so tightly that coloured circles begin dancing in the darkness. He takes the colours, mixes them, strokes them into lines, contours, heads, moves the brush, moves his shoulders, steps forwards and then a few steps backwards, moves back and forth in front of the canvas on the easel, ducks down and creeps around it, moves his shoulders, then stops perfectly still and touches the canvas over and over with the brush, breathing calmly in and out again, stroking and dabbing, a man with a dog's head holding a puppy to his chest with both hands, the pale pink of the tongue . . . He opens his eyes; the room is empty. And the stabbing is back in his chest straight away. No, not just in his chest; in his head, his stomach and in his legs and arms, but mainly in his chest. He's lying on his back, unable to move, looking up at the large chandelier. He threw a bottle at it, finest champagne, still half full, but he missed. That must have been a couple of hours ago, when he wasn't yet lying on the floor. He'd been lying in bed, a woman on either side of him. They'd been with him all day, massaging his arms and injecting him. They were naked and beautiful, and he'd stroked them cautiously a couple of times but there'd been no real point to it; he hadn't felt anything. They'd tried to fumble around at him but he'd just said, 'Don't,' and told them the rules. They started getting bored and he gave them a bit of coke, and later he asked them to get dressed again because he couldn't bear the two beautiful women so naked next to him and around him. 'One blonde, one brunette,' he'd said on the telephone, and when the guy had started talking about services he'd said, 'I don't care.'

The longing was still there sometimes, a little, especially when he woke up some time during the day, evening setting in again already, and he was suddenly very lucid and very alone.

He watched them getting dressed; the blonde had long hair that had covered her large breasts in bed beforehand, and a couple of times he'd grabbed her hair, enclosing a few strands in his fist so that only the tips were visible, and he stroked them across his face and the lids of his closed eyes like a brush.

'No,' he said, 'not everything, not everything please. Only your bras and underwear and your shoes.' By 'underwear' he meant their extravagant string tangas, but that kind of thing was presumably in right now and lots of young women wore that kind of 'underwear', but what did he know? And when they were lying next to him again, what a bed, what a huge, huge bed, and massaging his arms and injecting him in his left and right arms at the same time – 'My medication, they have to inject my medication, that's the only service I'm interested in, no matter what it costs' – he suddenly realised he'd painted all this before. Coloured pencil and pencil and watercolour on paper, forty-eight by sixty-nine centimetres, sold to a former film producer who'd bought the picture of the large shark tank before that and lived with a pile of money in a huge villa with lots of white walls. The big white bed. He was suddenly lying underneath a sheet; he'd pulled it up over his nose. 'Nose, nose,' he whispered into the sheet, breathing through the fabric. The brunette handed him the small silver tray he'd brought along specially, his lovely small silver tray, the blonde inserted the tube into his left nostril; the right one had been out of action for a good while now. He giggled into the sheet, and then he snorted and snorted until he no longer knew whether he'd painted all this before or would paint it in the future. And then he wasn't there at all any more, only two eyes watching everything he'd created, and if he hadn't created it yet . . . the blonde reared up, the silver tray so lopsided in her hand that the coke sprinkled like a fine white shower onto the sheet, underneath which Johannes Vettermann no longer existed. And the brunette lay next to her, wearing white fishnet stockings – 'Ladies, white is not a colour!' – lying strangely contorted on her side, and her arse looked monumental, two semi-circular and yet slightly angular rock formations, between them the equally white and so tiny piece of cloth of her panties (panties or tangas, at what width of fabric does the difference come in?), and the fishnet stockings weren't fishnet stockings either, they were ribbons crossing around her legs, and one of the ribbons snaked over her thighs and her arse . . . and Johannes Vettermann knows he'll have to force the matter soon, or no one will be interested in his monkey.

Oh yes, it's a particularly fine example squatting over there in the foreground. A mixture of orang-utan and gorilla with a gigantic head, a monkey with its eyes closed tight, not looking very happy. Oh no, thinks Johannes Vettermann under the white sheet and in front of the white easel, don't you three dare just disappear! He fences in the bed, fences in the two women and the monkey, but it's not a fence, it's ropes round a boxing ring – take a close look you idiots, can't you see the little boxing girl in the corner of the ring? And Johannes Vettermann knows he'll have to put some speed into it, he'll have to force things, and he knows that and he's lying under the sheet and sweating and sweating while the telephone rings.

He opens his eyes, sees the chandelier above him again, and the telephone rings. He smashes the telephone against the wall; the two women gather up the splinters of plastic from the bed; the ringing won't stop. And now he knows he has to pick up the receiver. He rolls onto his front, it hurts a lot, and then he crawls slowly towards the door. He feels his heart stumbling and breaking off, feels himself getting weaker and weaker; he's had so many heart attacks over the past few years. He crawls slowly, moving his arms, moving his legs, and the table with the telephone is still so far away. Why on earth did he take a large suite in the best hotel in town? A small, quiet double room would have done just as well. He hasn't got much money left now, but because he had so much money a few years ago he doesn't know what it's like to be economical. And two beautiful young women belong in a beautiful suite and not in a mid-range hotel with only beer and Coca Cola and apple juice in the mini-bar.

Johannes Vettermann crawls towards the telephone, not ringing any more now, he crawls and leaves a trail on the carpet. His nose is bleeding. But that doesn't bother him too much; his nose bleeds easily, his mucous membranes have been shot for years now, which bothers him a lot more and he finds slightly embarrassing even though the beautiful women are a thing of the past, but there's still always *something* or *somebody* there . . . Johannes Vettermann feels ashamed of his wet trousers and his clammy, warm legs. He feels the damp carpet beneath him and tries to crawl ahead faster. But there's something in his way, and he knows he won't get past it before he's eaten up what's lying on the carpet there ahead of him. Apples, bananas and oranges. He bites so hard into the peel of the banana that it splits open at the other end. 'Apples and pears, extra-large strawberries, oranges and satsumas and bananas, sweet peaches and melons, redcurrants and blackcurrants, kiwis and pineapples, cherries sweet and cherries sour, gooseberries! Vettermann's Fruit supplies everything young and fresh and well-grown at low prices!' He tries to punch his teeth into an apple but the banana has sapped all his strength, and he feels his heart stumbling, feels a pulsing in his head and a gigantic pressure behind his eyes, too much pressure on his blood vessels, and the blood-stained apple rolls across the carpet, and Johannes Vettermann crawls on slightly then lies still, ahead of him the fruit and next to him the shards of the glass bowl.

'Peaches are my favourite, father,' he says. His father puts the paper bag of fruit into his satchel, like every morning, and then puts two extra peaches on top. 'Peaches keep your skin fresh,' he says. And Johannes Vettermann, fifteen years of age, has very fresh and rosy skin that all the girls envy. 'Peaches keep your skin fresh,' he says and hands out peaches. In return, the girls let him draw them; he draws them while they eat his father's peaches. He draws the peaches too and his father. He draws all the fruit his father brings home with him. Sometimes his father takes him along to the wholesale fruit market, a huge hall full of crates, outside a huge yard full of crates, trucks arriving and unloading and driving away again, cooling rooms full of crates, sales counters across the entire hall, so much fruit, they supply the whole town with fruit, and his father takes him around everywhere, and most of all Johannes Vettermann likes sitting in the little office behind the pane of glass, where he can see the entire hall. He draws. Flies. He knows all sorts of flies. Big ones and small ones, the kind that only live very short lives and die on the old fruit, then there are green ones with long wings that shimmer in the glint of the strip-lighting. Sometimes he draws the flies larger than the fruit. Sometimes the flies are so big that they could grab the workers and fly off with them. He puts big spikes on their heads with which they could pierce through the workers. And he pierces through them. And then he hears them screaming. The flies and the workers. 'I'll give you as many peaches as you like if you take your clothes off.'

'You're crazy, Johnny.'

'No, you don't have to take everything off. Lie down on the bed over there, you can keep your underwear on.'

'No, Johnny.' Almost all of them call him Johnny, and he likes that; he loves John Lennon, he calls him Johnny too.

'I'll give you as many peaches and bananas as you like for a month.'

'But don't look at me so funny, Johnny.'

And Johannes Vettermann draws. Sometimes he stands for hours by the brightly coloured fruit and waits until the colours seep down into his head. He has oil paints in his bedroom too, but usually he just draws, pencil or charcoal, and leaves the colours in his head for now.

'What lovely skin you've got!' Johannes Vettermann,

sixteen years of age, is standing between the women in their brightly coloured dresses, patting his cheeks and stroking his hair. 'Peaches,' he says, but they're not interested in his fruit. They live in strange flats, and he stands at the big white walls and paints. Now the colours come from his head, he metes them out, sometimes forcing them back in again, and when he's not painting the walls he dances with the women and their men, who wear dresses just as brightly coloured and have hair just as long, dancing with them by the big walls – 'Johnny, Johnny, superstar!' – he coughs and smokes, takes what they give him, and he sees the colours and the flies and sees something else entirely, which scares him terribly, there's always *something* and *somebody* there, and he's scared even though he's dancing and laughing.

Johannes Vettermann notices he can no longer scream as there's no air left in his lungs, and he takes a hectic breath, inhales water and spits and coughs and tries not to drown. How could it have happened, how could the big glass front of the large aquarium just break? There are very high notes that can shatter glass; maybe the strange, thin woman standing there in front of the glass sang very high, but he didn't hear anything. Weren't there lots of tiny cracks in the glass beforehand? Did the sharks perhaps smash the glass themselves? What intelligent animals, attacking the places with the cracks over and over . . . Johannes Vettermann beats around himself with his arms, has to calm himself down, he knows that, has to try to float perfectly calmly on the water so he doesn't attract the sharks.

Which is worse, he thinks – drowning or being torn limb from limb by the sharks? 'Goodbye, Johnny, goodbye, Johnny, it was nice while it lasted . . . but sadly, sadly . . .'

Johannes Vettermann sees the sharks. There are red streaks on the water and now he feels the blood still flowing out of his nose. He has to stop the blood flow so he doesn't attract the sharks. He sees them, in a tight huddle a short distance away. They seem to be occupied with someone else. There's a big head floating on the water, shimmering white and pale blue, and strangely the water is almost transparent so Johannes Vettermann can make out the green surface beneath him. It's not a human head, he thinks. The empty eye sockets are huge, the mouth is an O, and the ears – he doesn't know anyone with ears that big. The head is bodiless, and now it submerges again and he watches it go. He's always imagined that people have to disappear into the sea, one day. I have to paint the sharks and the sea, he thinks, and then they're up close to him, he can feel their cold skin, he splutters and beats both arms against the carpet.

'Father,' he says, 'why haven't we got a house by the sea?'

'What would we want with the sea, son? What do you want with the sea?'

He knows his father is scared for him; all he does now is paint, paint and draw, and although he still eats the fruit and he still likes the taste his father knows something's changed. 'If you want,' says his father, 'if you absolutely have to go to the sea . . .'

But his father doesn't take him to the sea, doesn't

buy a house there either although that would have been an easy matter for him; business is going well. His father takes him to the art school, introduces him, his father has connections; business is going well. And Johannes Vettermann, seventeen years of age, stands facing the professors flicking through the portfolio of his drawings and pictures, and he sees gigantic insects above their heads. His father barricades him into a little room at the warehouse for a week, only fruit and steaks from the meat wholesaler next door. The foremen kept an eye out to make sure he didn't run away, didn't run to his painted walls where the women and men want to dance with him. So he danced on his own, in bed at night, there's always *something* and *somebody* there, and he heard them, the workers and the flies. And he imagined what it must be like to live in the sea.

'You have extraordinary talent, Mr Vettermann.'

'But you must bear in mind that it won't be easy.'

'And you'd be the youngest student at the academy.'

'But we have to be certain you're prepared to adapt a little here, after that school business . . .'

'I am prepared to,' says Johannes Vettermann; their heads are peaches and apples and over-ripe pears. On one of the pictures lying on the table in front of the professors is a man holding a huge, brown mosquito in one hand and plunging the insect's long sting into his arm, laughing, but his eyes are so vacant and white that the laugh is no longer a laugh.

'I want to join the family business, father, I want to earn money.'

'What about your pictures?'

'There are no more pictures in art now, father.'

And Johannes Vettermann, twenty-two years of age, first-class student at the academy, stands up on the bridge, below him the crates and the fruit and the workers, it's night, and the nights pass, and Capt'n Johnny sees all the colours, sees the fruit flowing, hears the workers and the trucks humming, it all disappears in his head and he doesn't let it out any more – 'There are no more pictures in art now, father.'

Some nights he thinks of picking up the brightly coloured fruit and putting it together, Mrs Apple and Mr Pear enjoying their evening off on a little wooden bench, and Mrs Pear wishing for nothing more than a particularly virile banana floating half-peeled above her, held by invisible threads. 'Johnny Vettermann, the wholesale fruit artist, supplies the best and freshest and sweetest installations!'

But who cares about what's been done before? Some nights on the bridge, the fruit flowing and the work humming below him, he still dreams of his apples and pears, bananas and peaches in New York and Paris, but then he thinks that it's action that counts.

And Johannes Vettermann lies naked on the load bed of a truck, parked outside a gallery whose owner he knows from art school, in the middle of one of the town's widest streets. He presses his face against the wood and can still smell the fruit and hears the slap of the whip, but he hardly feels the lashes, and later he looks in the mirror in surprise at his back, now scored with red welts. If he turns his head slightly he can make out the woman with the enraged face standing above him spread-legged, black leather and white fishnet stockings and her lovely skin. He hears cars beeping, voices, now and then calls; action, he thinks and presses his face back against the wood. And later, when the police turn up, he's happy.

The telephone rings. It rings and rings, and then it's silent for a moment, and then it rings again. Johannes Vettermann is sitting on a kind of podium on the pavement outside the gallery, speakers attached to his clothes, and he feels them vibrating; he's not listening to the voice any more, it's been saying the same sentences over and over for thirty or forty minutes but he's not sure about that, it might be over an hour now. All he sees is darkness; he's wearing two large eye patches that cover half his face. A slow and monotonous male voice, *his* voice, coming out of the speakers. He recited a couple of lines by an electronic band he likes listening to onto tape, and they've been playing in an endless loop along with a couple of recordings from the charity fair he and his father organised on the grounds of the wholesale fruit market. 'We're standing around and exhibiting ourselves. We're the shop-window dummies. We're the shop-window dummies. We're being watched and we're feeling our pulse. We're the shop-window dummies. We're looking around and we know it's a pose . . .' And the telephone rings and rings, 'Number thirteen please, who's got number thirteen, and the drum goes round and round, buy your raffle tickets, ladies and gentlemen.' And Johannes Vettermann, thirty-five years of age, is standing in amidst the brightly coloured people at the charity fair, he sees the children waving on the little wooden horses, it seems as if they were waving at him, and he clutches his tape recorder to his chest and sweats and he's scared. 'We're the shop-window dummies . . . We move around and we break the glass. We step outside and we walk round the town.' And Johannes Vettermann feels the monotonous voice on his body, and he imagines the crush of people staring and the police arriving, and he waits there in the dark behind the eye patches, and *something* and *someone* waits there with him. He feels as if strapped to the chair, isn't he strapped in, his feet and his shoulders? He lies still and can't move, but he doesn't want to get upset, he admitted himself voluntarily – 'Help me, please help me' – and he knows the flies and spiders and bugs will come to him; they love his sweat. He's never understood why insects are so crazy about opiates. He had a plate of heroin dregs in his flat. Flies and ants and spiders perched on the plate and around the plate. He feels the vibrations of the speakers on his body, the telephone still ringing in the background, everything arranged, voices and rings and a man who can only see the darkness. There are no more pictures in art now, father.

No one knows he's lying up here, twenty-seventh floor. Perhaps it's reception, room service or the hotel manager himself. Johannes Vettermann crawls slowly, one eye opened slightly, but everything around him is blurred and unfocused. All he knows is that he has to crawl towards the ringing. How often has he thought he was going to die, knew it and waited for it? But he survived every time. The good healthy fruit, he thinks, all the vitamins protected me all those years. And suddenly he's very warm, although he was freezing and shivering a moment ago, and he feels as if the hundreds and thousands of peaches, apples, bananas and kiwis he's eaten ever since he could eat, so for almost fifty years (and he ate them puréed too when he was a wee thing with no teeth), he feels as if now they were warming him and protecting him; their concentrate, or their souls, he thinks with a smile, he feels himself smiling, their souls are still inside him, and when one day in many years he's rotting in the ground the worms will come across a man made of vitamins, and they'll live a very healthy life down under the ground with him. Johannes Vettermann crawls across the five-star suite, he's crawled across so many five-star suites in his time, he's lain on the floor or in the bathtub, with water or without, he's looked out of the window, walls of glass, New York, London, Paris, Los Angeles, Mexico City. 1989 brought big money. Bananas and kiwis and oranges for the East. They had to buy new trucks to take the fruit to all the new places. We supplied the whole of the East, he thinks and now he feels that the telephone must be very near by, even though he can barely feel anything now and the ringing has stopped. It's perfectly silent in his suite; he doesn't even hear his own breathing.

'We're rich, Johannes.'

'Haven't we always been rich, father?'

'If you want to buy that house by the sea now, a villa for two million, we'll still have more than enough.' His father, who had started out over fifty years ago with a weekly market stall, is happy, standing with his son Johannes Vettermann, who hasn't painted a picture for over fifteen years, up on the bridge of the wholesale fruit market, and they watch the fruit flowing and they both laugh very loudly at the great flow of cash, holding each other by the shoulders. But Johannes Vettermann doesn't buy a house by the sea or a villa either. Johannes Vettermann buys pictures; suddenly he sees that there are pictures in art again, even if they're not his pictures. He buys pictures, pictures he doesn't understand at first, which he stands in front of and looks at for so long that he feels, it's coming to get me now.

And then Johannes Vettermann buys pictures, photographs, sculptures, installations; travels the world, dines out with artists in the finest restaurants, attends art auctions in tailor-made suits – 'Sculpture "Bunny". . . going once . . . going twice . . . does anyone bid more than number thirteen, the gentleman in the blue suit . . . and sold, "Bunny" goes to number thirteen for . . .' – and Johannes Vettermann sits in his spacious home, surrounded by pictures and photographs, and looks at 'Bunny', a white female torso sitting on a chair, no head, one long thin arm that looks very dead hanging down at the side of the chair, and her legs are as long and thin as locust legs. Two bent over, white sausages in the place where her head ought to be, bunny's ears, protruding behind the back of the chair like the handless arms of a strange puppeteer, *someone* and *something*, thinks Johannes Vettermann and strokes Bunny's black fishnet stockings on her thin legs. He sits with the woman who created her in a hotel room, wearing a vest and sweating and sweating and he feels the irregular beat of his heart. First he injected something to come up, a party, a reception and lots of people and lots of art, then he took something to come down, to find some kind of calm again, a long signal and a short one, no good for your ticker, it can be all over like a shot, that's how the film maker died who he admired so much, over ten years ago now. She's sitting by him on the bed, fully dressed, he puts his arm around her and presses his head against her shoulder, and she talks to him in a quiet voice, as if to a little child. 'All right, Johnny, it's all right.'

He had a girlfriend, he met her in Italy. He's a well-known art collector now, he's well-known for discovering young talents, and sometimes he wonders whether he'd have bought his own pictures, the ones he painted when he was young. 'You have extraordinary talent, Mr Vettermann.' He strokes Bunny and wonders whether he loved her, his Italian girlfriend, wonders whether he's ever loved anyone. He doesn't have children. He thinks of the sculpture of a pregnant woman he saw a few years ago. I have to meet the artist, he thought back then, and later he did meet him and bought other sculptures by him. The pregnant woman had one hand on her bump, one half of her body was grey, the other half exposed, without skin, so that you could see her yellowish skull, her muscle cords, the brownish tissue of her breast and the foetus and the umbilical cord inside her. Could I have had children? Could I have loved your mother, Bunny? He thinks of his mother; she died not long ago.

'Johannes.'

'Yes, mother?'

'Promise me you won't destroy yourself.'

'I promise, mother. I want to sell a lot more fruit and buy a lot more art.'

Johannes Vettermann, fifty-one years of age, is lying in his suite on the twenty-seventh floor and he can tell he's dying and he's trying to reach the telephone; the doctors have brought him back a couple of times before. A long signal and a short one. He's only creeping a centimetre at a time, although he knows he must be there any moment now. A long signal and a short one. He thinks of all the pictures he bought, of the celebrated exhibitions he put on with his collection, thinks of his own exhibitions in the past few years since he started painting again.

'Slit-eyed Charlie was the end and the beginning, right, Johnny?'

'Get out of here,' he whispers.

'The Vietcong is everywhere, right, Johnny?'

'Leave me alone,' he whispers, 'or help me.' He's not scared, even though the man standing in front of him looks like he's always imagined Mephisto. But this man is really his best friend, a painter he discovered and promoted and bought, and whom he once painted so that he looked like the devil himself.

'Start again, Johnny, you have to paint, paint, Johnny. Art, only art you make yourself can save you.' And Johannes Vettermann painted, even though he hadn't picked up a brush for almost twenty years. And now his friend Mephisto, the man who wanted to save him, is standing in front of him, blocking the last fifty centimetres to the telephone and saying things about the Viets. 'They were the end and the beginning, right, Johnny?'

And he's right; a couple of years after 1989 the Vietnamese started taking over the fruit market. They brought the prices down but he and his father didn't give up that quickly; they stood up on the bridge of the wholesale fruit market, swaying in the storm, gripping each other by the shoulders, and they were fearless and they knew they could be victorious, but the competition grew and grew – 'Vietnamese, Johnny, as if they came from China' – and the prices fell and fell, and Vettermann's wholesale fruit market went bust, and his father, who'd started out with a weekly market stall over fifty years ago, turned into a broken old man, and they sat in banks and financial institutions and watched the red grow and grow. 'The colours, Johnny, never forget the colours . . .'

'And another painting from the Vettermann Collection, ladies and gentlemen, at a starting price of . . .' Johannes Vettermann had paid far less for the picture. It's his favourite picture and he sorely misses it. A man standing in a boat, fishing. The colours of the water and the sky are very pale, violet and blue, mist on the water, and the man stands dark like a shadow, and behind him on the banks the shadow of the forest. Neo-romantic, almost kitsch, Johannes Vettermann thought at first, but then after a while he was still standing in front of the picture and he began to feel the loneliness and the beauty.

Now it belongs to a Parisian collector, and once when Johannes Vettermann was in Paris he visited him and stood a long time looking at the angler and the forest and the water.

Almost all the pictures in his collection were auctioned off for a lot of money; Berlin, London, New York; the wholesale fruit market and the bridge where he'd stood for so many years were gone but so were the debts, and Johannes Vettermann gave up eating fruit.

'Paint, you have to paint again, Johnny . . .' And he painted. The end and the beginning. It took quite a long time until he managed to get the pictures out of his head and onto canvas. And it took quite a long time until the critics, the collectors and the other painters started celebrating him.

'Hell on canvas. The genius nightmares of Johannes Vettermann.'

And now here's his friend, the man he painted to look like Mephisto, like the devil himself in human form, standing in front of him and saying, 'Johnny Superstar' and 'At the end, Johnny, everything goes very fast,' and then he's gone. And Johannes Vettermann finally reaches for the receiver and presses it to his ear. But all he can hear is a very loud and never-ending beep, beep, beep, beep . . .

A TRIP TO THE RIVER

We called him 'The Boxer' because his nose was beaten so flat it almost disappeared into his face.

Sometimes when I sat with him by the window in the evening and we smoked in the floodlights and waited for the night, he laid his big hand across his battered face and left it there until we got up and went to our beds.

We had plenty of beaten-up guys. I saw them at work, I saw them in the corridors and the yard; there were some who came in with really pretty faces and went out mashed up, but in all my time I never saw a nose flat as the Boxer's.

At night, when I lay awake and he was asleep, his nose made whistling sounds, and when I listened for a while and thought about things, they'd turn into real little tunes.

'Hey, Boxer, play something else,' I said quietly, but he stopped whistling altogether – he'd woken up and started tossing and turning above me. 'You know,' he whispered in his hoarse night voice, 'you know, I really used to . . . back then . . .'

151

'Yeah,' I said, 'that's what they're all saying. This guy came in last week, short guy, going a bit grey . . .'

'Wolfgang,' he whispered.

'Yeah,' I nodded a couple of times, even though he couldn't see me.

'Always was a big-mouth,' he whispered.

He turned over above me. I saw his foot for a moment in the light of the prison moon; we hung our towels over the window, but the floodlights were in the yard and outside the walls, and we never managed to completely cover it. I heard him breathing, and a few minutes later he started up his whistling again.

'He weren't bad,' Wolfgang had said, passing round cigarettes, he was shit-scared, 'back in the East. Not right at the top, but a couple of times he nearly made it to the Olympics a couple of times.'

The Boxer had never told me that, even though we'd been sharing a cell for more than two years. The Boxer didn't talk much, and once he did get started, because the Russkis had brought us some *samogon*, he used to tell me about his daughter. She must have been seventeen, eighteen.

He still had a few years to go. They said he'd knocked some guy out and he hadn't got up again, in the pub, a fight, money, women, no one knew exactly and of course he'd never told anyone anything.

One of the old dossers, who came and went, and were all back inside again for the winter, even told me once the Boxer was a lifer, on a long stretch. Apparently he hadn't just knocked out that one guy but beat a security man into a coma too when he tried to hold him down, and he slept so deep he never woke.

'The Boxer lost it; it was the drink,' the dosser said and shook his head and rolled his eyes enough to make me dizzy. 'They got him down to ten or eleven years; it was the drink, you know.'

'I know,' I said, and the old guy licked his lips and I gave him a bit of tobacco. But I didn't believe the Boxer was carrying *two* cold ones round with him, and the tramps talked a lot of shit when they were coming down.

'They should have built it by the river,' the Boxer said. We were sitting at the table, like every morning. It was slowly getting light outside; the window was open although it was cold and it had snowed. We were eating and looking out across the walls at the bare trees and the city. 'What?' I asked, although I knew what he meant. He tapped one of the bars, and I nodded. 'Might have been better.'

'The view, you know.' He pushed his plate aside and got up. 'You know, a river, when you can see it all the time, on a river there's always something going on.' I got up as well and stood next to him, and we looked out at the buildings, a long way off, that the river must have been behind somewhere. He did us two roll-ups and passed me one. 'You gonna look at it?'

'The river?' I gave him a light and he nodded.

'Maybe,' I said.

'Gonna get your leave after all, eh?'

'Looks like it. But you never know with them.'

'You gonna go on a trip?'

'It's only a weekend.'

'I mean a *real* trip.' He looked at me and I saw a thin trail of smoke coming out of one of his nostrils, now just a slit.

'Nah, they always find you anyway. A trip . . .' I laughed, and he smiled too and flicked his roll-up out between the bars.

'So . . . so d'you wanna go anywhere, got any plans?'

'This and that,' I said, 'Leipzig, the usual, you know.'

'Our city,' he said. I stubbed my rollie out in the snow on the windowsill. He rolled two more, lit them up and passed me one.

'Wanna visit your sister, eh?'

'Nah, better not. She's just got married.'

'Kid?'

'Yeah. Still a littl'un.'

'When my daughter . . .' He flicked his half-smoked roll-up out the window and closed it. I picked up the ashtray from the table and lay down on my bed. 'You know your leave . . .' The Boxer turned round to me for a moment, then he leant his forehead against the window pane. I smoked and looked at his back. It was a pretty broad back; maybe he'd been a cruiserweight, maybe even one class higher, in his golden days, when he'd nearly made it to the Olympics. I dragged on my rollie until I felt the heat on my lips. 'When you're out on leave . . .' the Boxer said, muffled against the glass and moving his head back and forth. I pressed the butt into the ashtray, the key banged in the lock, the Boxer turned to face the door, I jumped up, the ashtray fell on the floor, I nudged it under the bed with my foot. The warden was standing in the door, seven a.m., time for work.

'When you're out on leave,' said the Boxer in the middle of the night, when he woke up, 'You listening . . . ?' I didn't answer, I didn't breathe, but he kept on talking because he knew I was awake. '. . . And when you're in the city, in Leipzig . . . you know, son . . .' I hated it when he called me 'son'. I'd celebrated my thirtieth with him last summer. He'd got hold of some *samogon* and home brew from the Russians, and then he'd spent all night talking about his daughter until he fell asleep. 'Got such dark hair, nearly black, not from her mother, no. Had it down over her shoulders, back then, you know . . . And take a good look what she looks like now, you listening son, take such a good look that . . . How tall she is and that, her eyes, her eyes as well . . .' He came down the ladder, I saw him dark in front of my bed. I sat up and leant against the wall. 'Course,' I said, 'I'll tell you all about her eyes, if that's all you want.'

'Something else,' he said, and I heard him walking across the dark cell to the table and sitting down. His lighter clicked, and then I saw the burning tip of his cigarette moving to and fro as he spoke. 'There's these two poofters owe me something. Won't be any trouble. Got a little shop. Beer, schnapps, herring rolls. I'll let them know you're coming. It's not much. Take it and give it to her. S'a surprise. She's on a training scheme, not much coming in. I trust you. And tell her . . . tell her . . .'

'I'll tell her, Boxer.' I leant against the wall, pulled the blanket up and over my head and breathed through the material.

The Boxer was standing at the window. But when I

looked up at him and raised my hand briefly, I wasn't so sure any more, so far away, and the twisted wire between us on top of the wall. I looked at the big clock on the tower, ten to eleven, same as always. I noticed it was snowing, and wiped the snow off my hair. Then I walked slowly away from the gate, turned around again, saw the woman behind the glass of the porter's lodge, old and white-haired – been here since Adolf, we used to say. I walked past the little shop, closed now, saw the original jailbird products in the window: guaranteed organic potatoes, wooden figures, baskets, *my* baskets; I'd got to be a great basket-weaver during my time. I stood still by the commemorative plaque in the little car park a few yards away from the shop. 'In memory of the victims of the fascist dictatorship in Fort Zinna.' Someone had laid flowers in the snow. There was another commemorative stone a bit further along, because the Russkis had been here too. When I first arrived I'd walked to and fro between the stones until it got dark and I went up to the gate. I put my bag down and looked past the jail to the fields. I lit up and squatted down. I pressed my hand into the snow and felt it melting between my fingers and kept looking at the white fields and dragging on my roll-up, until I noticed the snow had put it out. I wiped my wet hand across my face and got up. I threw the roll-up away and walked towards the bus stop. I passed the low building where the day-release boys lived. Two of them were standing outside and nodded at me. I raised my hand briefly, fingers slightly apart – that was how we used to put them on windows, doors, walls. When I turned round again a few yards later they were still watching me go, hands in their pockets.

'Drinks World,' 'Sports Corner,' 'Torgau welcomes careful drivers'. The bus drove so fast I felt sick, but I knew it would get slower the further we drove. Someone once told me he'd had to puke the first time he got on a bus after five years.

I felt people looking at my bag and staring at me and leant my head on the window. When we drove past the brewery I wanted to get out, but I stayed put. The bus stopped at a crossroads and I saw the sign 'Riesa 182 km' next to me. There was a big juvenile facility there, out in Zeithain, in the middle of nowhere, but I was a few years too old for them now. 'How much time you done now, son?' asked the Boxer.

'It's been a few years now,' I said, 'all together.'

'Can't grumble either,' said the Boxer. We were playing chess and I offered him a pawn. He ate it up, and a few moves later his king got what was coming to him. It was only boxing he'd been top-class at. I'd learned to play chess more than ten years ago in Zeithain. 'Traudi's Inn'. I got out. The station was one stop away, but the trains to Leipzig ran all day, and I went in to see Traudi. The door swung to behind me, and I opened it again and looked out. The bus was driving down the road and I saw a couple of heads moving behind the big rear window. 'Hey, it's getting cold,' someone said, and I flinched, dropped my bag and turned around. Just an old bloke at one of the tables, holding tight to a beer bottle with both hands and looking down at the tabletop, pretty far gone. I picked up my bag and went up to the bar. Some scrawny guy was fiddling with the beer pumps, but when I sat down on one of the bar stools I saw that the scrawny guy had a truckload of lipstick on and must have been a woman. As if she wanted to prove it, she stuck out her chest and smiled. She had a name-tag on her apron, it said, 'Traudi Schmidt at your service'.

They talked about *Big* Traudi inside, 'Got this great place, you gotta go there when you get out, Big Traudi's got the best beer in town, you better believe it,' but perhaps Big Traudi had been on a diet over the years. 'All right,' I said.

'Beer and a shot, right?' she said and smiled and looked at my bag and curved her scrawny back so far forwards I started worrying about her spine.

'Coffee,' I said, and she turned round and got to work on the coffee machine. I went through my pockets and put a tenner down on the bar. 'Can you change this for me?'

Traudi put my coffee down next to the note. 'No problem,' she said and took it. She held the tenner between her forefinger and thumb and fanned it in front of her face and smiled at me as if she'd been in another kind of business, back when she was fat. I unwrapped the sugar cube, dipped it in the coffee and watched it slowly dissolve. Traudi was still grinning at me and now she stroked her lips with the note. I drank a mouthful of my coffee, then I poured in some milk and stirred it around a couple of times with the spoon. 'How d'you want it?' asked Traudi and looked at me over the note.

'For the machine,' I said. She screwed up the tenner in her fist and bent over to the till. She fingered through the coins and slapped three twos and four ones down on the counter. I nodded and went over to the cigarette machine. The old bloke looked up for a moment, still clinging onto the beer bottle, empty now. He really did look pretty far gone, like the alkies and dossers inside when they couldn't get hold of any home brew. Some of them tried to make their own, and collected every crust of bread and every rotten apple they could get, but most of them had the DTs and messed it up.

'A beer,' said the old man, 'a nice cold beer. And a shot, you know. You'll think of me, won't you, drink one for me?'

'Yeah, right,' I said, 'a double just for you. Soon as I get to the station.' The old guy smiled, and for a second his head stopped wavering and even his eyes were still. The coins jangled through the machine and I selected my old brand. I had to put more money in; the prices had gone up. I leant over and picked up the packet. I looked around. Traudi had poured herself a beer and was drinking and flicking through a thick catalogue in front of her on the counter. Looked like underwear and clothes.

'Mate, got one for me?' The old man looked at me, lowered his head slightly and let go of his empty bottle. I put the new packet in the inside pocket of my jacket and gave the old man four of the roll-ups the Boxer had given me that morning, 'For the journey, son.' He smoked the cheapest stuff, we called it 'pubes', but some evenings, when we were sitting at the window and waiting for the night and swapping cigarettes, his roll-ups tasted better than Davidoff Filter. I paid for my coffee and left.

I saw four chemist shops by the time I got to the station, three of them on the same road. Maybe people in Torgau were really run-down and got ill easily, or they beat each other up all the time and needed loads of bandages.

There were a couple of people in the ticket office so I got

my ticket from a machine. The station pub didn't open till the evening, and I stood in front of the timetable and smoked and read the names of the towns, until they announced my train and I noticed I was cold and felt a bit sick. On the platform was a girl with a dog. Fairly pretty even, maybe a bit too young, seventeen or eighteen, dark hair and nearly black and down over her shoulders, and her eyes . . .

The little grey dog danced around her, and she took a couple of steps so the lead didn't get tangled around her legs. I dropped my bag and squatted down as the little grey dog danced in my direction and stopped a couple of yards in front of me; maybe the lead wasn't long enough or she was pulling him back. But I didn't even see her any more, although she was really quite pretty; there was only the little grey dog in front of me, in the middle of the platform. He raised his head and sniffed, his nose was shiny. I held out my palm to him, my fingers slightly apart, the dog danced to and fro a bit and howled quietly. I heard the train pulling in and straightened up.

And then night. In fact it was still evening, but it had been dark since four, and I saw all the bright lights of the city. I stood outside the door, looked at the cars driving by, looked at the luminous signs and windows of the shops and bars opposite. The Turks and the Arabs had taken the area over years ago, and the Russians had a hand in things too, and back then before I went inside I'd had a couple of run-ins on this street, when we crawled from one bar to the next, but that was all over now. I opened the door and went inside. I took the money out of my bag, counted it out, rolled it up and put it in my inside pocket. The money smelled of fish, and the two queers in their little snack bar had stunk of fish as well.

'The Boxer sent you, did he? Shacked up with him, are you?'

The guy winked at me and leaned over the little counter. 'Used to look out for me, always looked out for me back then.' He talked about their great friendship, about the Boxer's honour, 'Never lets anyone down, never leaves you in the lurch, you better believe it,' and he talked about how the Boxer nearly made it to the Olympics, back then. He put a can of beer down in front of me and opened one for himself. 'Have a drink. Out on leave, are you? Let's drink to the Boxer.' We said cheers, and he started talking again, about the Boxer and about the jail and about their golden days. The other queer didn't say a word the whole time and just cut rolls and herrings, and when he started on the onions and queer number one was still going on and on, I flicked my half-smoked roll-up across the counter at him and said: 'Time's up.' He grinned and nodded and took me to a little caravan he called 'my office', and it stank of fish and beer and cigarettes in there too.

I walked slowly up the stairs. The house was silent, and when the light went off I stood still and lit up. I walked on slowly in the dark. Light shone through the pane in the door. I stood still and put my hand on the bars. 'Close it, I wanna show you something.' I closed the window, turned around and still felt the bars cold on my hand. The Boxer was standing naked to the waist in front of his bed. 'Hey, what's this all about, pal?'

161

'Just wanna show you something, son, come over here, come closer.' He'd put his big hand on his chest, and I walked over to him slowly. He had the usual words and pictures on his arms and a big eye in the middle of his belly, but I'd seen all that often enough in the two years we'd been sharing. The Boxer wasn't quite as inked up as the billboards I used to see in the showers, who carried their whole lives around with them on their skin, but he went to one of our in-house tattooists every couple of months. 'It's a new one, you haven't seen it yet, it's still fresh. Don't need no photo any more. Never. Chucked them all away. She'll always be with me now.' He took his hand off his chest. There was the face of a young woman, she had shoulder-length black hair and was smiling. Her eyes were much too big, almost like in Japanese comics. She must really have been pretty fresh; her face was swollen up, especially her forehead and below her mouth – there weren't any tattoo care sets in Fort Zinna. 'Looks really beautiful,' I said, and the Boxer nodded and went a bit red. I looked at his daughter, smiling at me with her big eyes. 'Come in,' she said. I looked at her nose, then her hair, which was quite short, and then her eyes . . . now they were sparkling and squinting at me. 'Come in,' she said again, 'come on in if you're going to.' She turned around and I followed her along the hall. Maybe the Boxer had told her I was coming, maybe the herring boys. 'The door,' she said, and I went back again and closed it.

She sat down on the sofa. I stayed standing up in front of her, and she squinted up at me so that I took a couple of steps back. I held onto my bag with both hands and looked around. It all looked pretty cheap, but the Boxer had told me she was doing some training course, as a hotel clerk or something. 'Like a drink?' I nodded. She went past me to the sideboard, and behind me I heard her clinking glasses. She took a couple of steps, and then I felt her breath on the back of my neck. I held onto my bag and looked at the wall above the sofa. There was some reproduction modern picture up there, all just blobs of colour. She walked slowly back to the sofa and put two glasses of brown liquor on the table. 'Why don't you sit down,' she said. She stroked the sofa cushions and tilted her head and smiled; she must have learnt that on her course.

I put my bag down and sat down next to her. 'You've come on a little trip because of me, right?' she said and moved closer. 'Not that far,' I said. I picked up my glass; it smelled like cheap and nasty 'Goldbrand', tasted like it too.

'Bet you're glad you're here now, right?' She moved away from me again towards the armrest, kicked off her shoes and stretched out her legs, touching my knees with her feet. I reached for my glass and pushed it to and fro on the table. There was an ashtray there as well, and I pulled out my cigarettes. I felt the roll of money in my inside pocket. 'Be a sweetie and give us one.' I lit my cigarette and handed her the packet. She fingered one out and put the packet down on her leg. I wanted to give her a light, but she took the cigarette out of my mouth and lit hers on it. I stood up and reached into my inside pocket. 'Listen . . .'

'Hey, don't go running off.' She jumped up so quickly that her cigarette and my cigarette and the packet as well fell on the carpet, but she took no notice and pressed right up to me and put her arms around me. She was really strong, even though she was so short. I wanted to push her away, throw the money on the table and disappear, find a place to hide and wait for Monday, but she held tight; she must have got her strength from the Boxer.

'Don't do that,' I said, but she was still hanging on to me and rubbing her face against my neck, it must have been her nose, no, she can't have got that from the Boxer, but maybe he'd had the best nose in town, *before* he nearly made it to the Olympics. She fumbled with my flies and said, 'You've got to give me something, you know . . .'

I felt the roll of money in my inside pocket, but I knew that wasn't what she meant, and now I knew that neither the Boxer nor the herring boys had told her I was coming either. I grabbed her by the shoulders but let her go again straight away, because I felt her skin and bones. I picked up my half-empty glass and lobbed it at the sideboard, so hard that splinters of glass and drops of liquor sprayed back at us. She took a couple of slow steps away from me and looked at me with her big Japanese comic eyes. I stumbled backwards and sat down on the sofa. I picked up her glass and drank it dry. Suddenly there was a man in the middle of the room. 'Trouble,' he said and came over to me. He walked fairly slowly, and I could have got him in the face with the glass, but I put it down on the table. I got up. I saw him pulling back to punch, but I didn't move. He had a good right hook and I was on the floor. I turned on my side and looked between the table legs. She was crouching in front of the sideboard, her chin on her knees, and I looked her straight in the face. I got up.

Straight away, the guy gave me two or three hard ones, and I went down again and looked under the table at the Boxer's daughter, still crouched in front of the sideboard, not moving. I felt blood on my face. I saw the guy's legs right next to me, I could have grabbed them, pulled him over and mashed him up, but I got up again and looked at him. He didn't hit me straight away, and I looked over his shoulder at the wall. The guy rammed his knee in my belly, I gasped for breath and crouched down.

'Stay down, fucker.' He punched like a professional and talked like one too. I lifted my head slightly and saw her leaning forwards and moving both hands to and fro over the carpet, as if she was playing with something. I got up slowly and closed my eyes. He got me pretty bad, and I felt my nose break.

'Hey son,' said the Boxer, 'you're nearly as pretty as me.'

'Walked into a door,' I said, 'in town. The usual, you know.'

'Did she see you like that? You didn't scare her?'

'No no, Boxer, I went to hers first, it was all all right. She's fine. She was pleased, the money and that, really pleased.'

'Wasn't much, but she's still a trainee, in a real hotel. She doesn't get much there, has to watch her money.'

'I know.'

I stood on the bridge and looked down at the river. In the fields on either side were the remains of the morning mist. I heard the cars behind me, quite a lot of traffic, start of the week. A long way off, I saw a tugboat on the wide river. It didn't seem to be moving. Maybe it was going over to the

Czechs, maybe in my direction and then on to the sea in Hamburg. I lit up my last filter cigarette and threw the empty packet in the river. My nose started bleeding again, and I pulled a tissue out of my inside pocket. It smelled of fish, just like the money. I'd put it in her letterbox on the ground floor. Really wasn't much, just over a ton, but it must have been the Boxer's last reserves from his golden days, when he nearly made it to the Olympics. I looked down at the river again. A couple of ice chunks disappeared under the bridge. One got caught up on a red marker buoy, then broke free and floated on again. I pressed the tissue to my nose, threw my fag-end in the river and went home.

IN THE AISLES

Before I became a shelf-stacker and spent my evenings and nights in the aisles of the cash-and-carry market, filling shelves, fetching pallets from high on the storage shelves with the forklift, now and then helping one of the last customers of the evening and getting to know all kinds of food, I'd been working on building sites for a couple of years.

I hadn't given up of my own accord but I wouldn't have kept it up all that long, even if the boss hadn't fired me. I was a builder's mate, lugging sacks of cement and plasterboard, gutting flats – that meant I knocked the plaster off the walls, tore out fireplaces and chimneys with a big sledgehammer we used to call 'Rover', until I was covered in soot and dirt and spent hours getting the soot and dust out of my nose at home. The firm didn't even pay well and the boss was a bastard. The guy came from Bavaria; I've met people from Bavaria who were actually OK though.

I can't remember exactly when all the fuss with the

boss started, but I do know we were demolishing an old roof that day. We found a big pigeon's graveyard, two pigeons still alive and perfectly still in among all the bones, piles of feathers and pigeon shit and decomposing and mummified corpses, and we could only tell by their eyes and their heads, moving slightly every now and then, that they were waiting. We fetched the Portuguese guys and they killed them with a blow of a spade. Then we tipped lime over the pigeon grave-yard and shovelled it all into buckets and tipped them down the rubbish chute fastened to the scaffolding outside.

And after that we didn't feel much like hard work any more; the pigeons had got to us. We took the tiles off another section of the roof, not exactly motivated, removed the roof battens with wrecking bars, and then we took a lunch break.

We usually had our lunch break at eleven thirty, and when the bells of the church just round the corner rang at twelve we went back to work.

But when the bells rang that day we were still sitting with the Portuguese guys. They were drinking red wine out of cartons, passing them around. The Portuguese guys spoke very bad German and earned even less than we did and lived in tiny basement flats in one of the buildings owned by the boss. They drank red wine at work because they knew the boss wouldn't fire them – they worked too well for too little money. They did bricklaying and plastering, and sometimes they were builder's mates like us, lugging sacks of cement, gutting flats until they were covered in soot and dust.

And then when the fuss with the boss started and I'd

slapped him round the face on both sides with my cement-encrusted glove, they all came to me one after another and shook my hand, pressed it and pumped it, said, 'You did good thing' in broken German, laughed and said, 'You find new job, you good worker,' and patted me on the back.

'Lazy bastard,' the boss had called me, and I hadn't even been holding a wine carton any more, I was just sitting on an upturned bucket and leaning on the wall and trying to think of nothing at all.

And I wasn't a lazy bastard, even if I had overdone it a bit with my lunch break.

And when I started the job as a shelf-stacker in the cash and carry they noticed straight away that I wasn't a lazy bastard. I'd got the job through someone I knew, a guy who'd been working there for four years.

I'd got him a job seven or eight years ago and he knew I'd been out of work since the fuss at the building site, so when a job came up in the 'Shelf-filling/Night' department he'd put my name down for it. I made a real effort, stacking the stock on the shelves where they showed me, pulling a large barred cart along behind me to put empty cartons and packaging into. They explained how to use the little manual pallet jacks for lifting and moving pallets of stock around. They had electric pallet jacks too, called 'ants', for transporting several pallets stacked up, but I wasn't allowed to use those ones yet.

It wasn't one of those cash-and-carries that anyone could shop at. The customers had to have a special card; they had to run a company, self-employed people and that kind of thing who were buying for their businesses. We had a food section and a non-food section, but I was only ever on food and beverages. It was a huge market, on two floors with clothing and electronics upstairs. The food section was on the lower floor, and made up of different departments like Processed Food, Confectionery, Frozen Food, Delicatessen, Fruit and Vegetables and a couple of other ones I can't remember now.

The aisles between the shelves were very wide so there was space for the forklifts. The forklifts operated all day long, even when the market was open for customers. The forklift drivers fetched large pallets out of the storage shelves, which went right up to the ceiling on top of the normal shelves where the customers took the stock from and put it in their trolleys.

To start with I was always wondering why there weren't any terrible accidents, why no pallets tipped off the forks and crushed ten customers to death, why no feet got squashed under the large iron wheels of the forklifts. But later, when I had a forklift licence of my own and whizzed along the aisles in my yellow forklift, fetching pallets of beer or milk or sacks of flour down from the shelves, I knew it was all a matter of relaxing, taking care and judging distances right – and routine. But the most important thing, I thought, was that you had to be absolutely convinced while you were transporting pallets up or down that you were the very centre of the market.

It took me a while to learn how to drive a forklift. They let me do my practice after opening hours, when the only people in the aisles were from 'Shelf-filling/Night'. One of the long-term staff was a registered examiner, but another long-term guy gave me practice lessons until I'd managed to learn all the secrets of driving and operating a forklift. Actually it was just the half-hour before the end of our shift at one a.m. Under his supervision, I drove his forklift – which I shared with him later – slowly along the aisles, stopped in the right position parallel to the shelf, positioned the fork and moved it upwards. Then when the fork was at the level of the pallet I steered the truck until the ends of the fork were just above the openings in the pallet. Then I pressed a lever on the control panel in front of me, and the fork lowered and slipped into the openings in the pallet. Then I pressed the other lever and the pallet rose slowly.

'You're doing well,' said Bruno, his big hand next to me on the control panel, 'just don't raise it too quickly or you'll bump it at the top.'

Bruno was a pretty tall, stocky man, actually more stocky than tall, probably in his mid-fifties with white hair, but when you saw him from a distance he looked like a wrestler or a heavyweight boxer. He had a big block of a head that perched directly on his shoulders, almost no neck at all between the lapels of his white overall, and his hands, one of which was now resting on the forklift control panel next to me, were the size of plates. He wore a broad leather cuff around his right wrist to protect his tendons. He worked in the beverages department, where they fetched the largest pallets down from the shelves – crates of beer and juice and other drinks, which were roped together but still swayed ominously to and fro on the pallet as we lowered them out of the shelves.

Bruno had been working in the cash and carry for over ten years, always on beverages, and even though he wasn't the department manager it was him who kept the place running.

'You're doing well, Lofty,' he said. 'You'll soon have your licence.' He called me Lofty, like most of my workmates did, because I was nearly six foot three.

'Forget it,' I said. 'I know I'm making a mess of it.'

He laughed. 'Oh, don't worry. The longer it takes, the better for me. I have a nice quiet time with you. Better than all that hard graft.' He pointed a thumb over at the beverages section. I heard bottles clinking through the shelves. Another workmate was lugging the last crates of the day.

'There was one time,' said Bruno, watching me attempt to get a pallet of salt boxes back onto the shelf, 'one time I dropped a load of beer. Couple of years ago now. The rope tore. Shit happens.' He reached into the pocket of his overall and took out a couple of ropes. He never threw them away when we cut them off the big beer pallets with our Stanley knives once we'd got them down in one piece. 'Always come in handy.' He had a little farmyard outside of town, with a stable and a few animals. He lived there with his wife; she took care of the animals and everything else while he was at work. Bruno always had this special smell to him, of animals and manure, but it wasn't as if he stank; he just smelt faintly, and there was something else in the mixture that he brought along from his farm, something strangely sweet, more like bitter-sweet, but I never worked out what it might be.

'Bring her down now,' said Bruno, checking his watch, 'time to clock off.'

'OK,' I said. I'd finally managed to get the salt pallet in the right gap. I extracted the fork, moved the truck back slightly, then pressed one of the levers and the fork came down very slowly from the very top, with a hissing and whooshing sound from the air expelled from the hydraulics. I waited until the fork touched the tiled floor and then positioned it so that the forks weren't parallel to the ground. 'Only drive with the forks tipped, never with the fork raised except when you're stacking.'

I'd had to watch a couple of instruction films where they listed all these terrible accidents as a deterrent and then showed some of the consequences. Lopped-off limbs, flattened feet, people skewered on the fork, and the more I saw of this forklift inferno, the more often I wondered if I'd chosen the right job. But the other staff at the cash and carry were nice enough, and I didn't intend to skewer them on the fork or drive over their feet.

'Are you coming, Bruno?'

'No, you drive it on your own, you know how to do it now.' Sometimes Bruno stood on the tipped forks, even though that wasn't allowed, and rode back to the recharging station with me. I drove off and saw him walking down the aisle in the other direction. He walked slightly hunched, his arms splayed a little way from his body as if he expected a surprise attack from one of the shelves at any moment. I tried to imagine him working on the building site with me, me explaining everything to him and showing him how to do the job, but I just couldn't imagine the man demolishing a roof. Maybe it was his white hair, and that smell of his animals didn't go with the dust.

I drove to the recharging station, right at the back of the warehouse by the delivery bay. I drove along the empty, brightly lit aisles, past the freezers and the long rows of refrigerated shelves against the walls. Ours was the last shift and I only saw a workmate now and then. They were standing in the aisles, doing their last chores, standing at the blue wheeled desks and writing lists of the damaged or torn-open stock we always found on the shelves; others were getting their forklifts ready for the night at the recharging station. I didn't know all of their names yet, and even later, once I'd been working at the warehouse for a while and had scraped through the forklift test ('It'll end in tears, Lofty'), I took a shifty look at the name tags on their overalls when I talked to them or needed help.

'Thanks, Ms Koch,' I said, and she smiled and said, 'No problem.'

I saw her looking at my overall, but I'd lost my name tag and hadn't got a new one yet.

'Christian,' I said and gave her my hand. 'Marion,' she said. She'd lent me her forklift because a customer had asked for a bottle of Wild Turkey just before closing time. I'd fetched the whisky pallet down from the shelf, given him the bottle and then filled up the empty compartment. Bruno was using our forklift over in the beer section. It was a Friday, it was summer, and people were buying beer by the crateload.

'Shall we have a coffee? It's on me.'

'OK,' she said, and then we went to the vending machine. There were two coffee machines in the warehouse, one at the delivery bay and one in front of the cold storage room, and that one was closer.

I'd come across her in the aisles a couple of times before and we'd nodded hello, and seeing as she was quite pretty I'd smiled every time.

She wasn't there every night, she worked days as well; only me and five other guys were always on nights.

'You did your test quite quickly.' She sipped at her coffee, and then she blew into the little clouds of steam. She smiled; she'd probably heard about how much trouble I'd had with it.

'Bruno was a good teacher,' I said and looked at the name tag on her chest again. 'M. Koch, Confectionery'.

'Bruno's a good guy,' she said. 'You can always go to him when you need help, or when you're fed up and you fancy a coffee and a chat.' She smiled and blew into her coffee, then she drank a few mouthfuls.

'Get fed up often, do you?'

'Don't be so cheeky, rookie.' She held her coffee in front of her name tag and tapped me on the shoulder with the index finger of her free hand. Then she laughed, and I couldn't help joining in. There was something about her and the way she talked to me that I liked a lot. When I'd sat down in her forklift ('But don't make a tour of it, I need it back again') I'd felt the warmth on the seat where she'd just been sitting.

She seemed to be a couple of years older than me,

maybe in her mid-thirties. She had quite short hair that was always kind of messy. We drank our coffee and talked about this and that.

We stood at the vending machine for a long time, and I kept putting more money in and refilling our cups. We were standing behind the piles of crates and stock so the only people who could see us were people who wanted to take a coffee break of their own. 'Be right back.' I went to the shopping trolley containing food just coming up to the best-before date. Sometimes there were three or four trolleys, and sometimes it was my job to take the trolleys to the ramp by the delivery bay where the rubbish bins were. Bread, chocolate, meat, milk, all still good for a few more days, and if I was hungry I tried to sneakily stuff myself with as much as possible of the best things before I threw them in the bins. Chocolate truffles, ciabatta with Serrano ham, Kinder chocolate. If one of the bosses caught me I could take off my overalls and leave, but I just couldn't resist it. The stuff was being chucked out anyway, and I think most of us took the odd sneaky helping.

I tore open the packaging of a chocolate cake, cut two large slices with my Stanley knife, put them in the pockets of my overalls and went back over to Marion.

'I thought you'd had enough of me.'

'No,' I said, 'not at all. Hold out your hand.' She gave me a questioning look but then held her hand out flat, and I took a piece of cake out of my pocket and placed it on her hand. 'Hey, rookie,' she said, 'you're a bit of a daredevil, aren't you?'

It wasn't until later that I thought I'd actually put her at risk. If they'd caught us . . . but we were safe behind the crates, and anyway the big bosses had left ages ago and the boss of 'Shelf-filling/Night' was pretty relaxed and often disappeared to the toilets for a quick smoke, even though it wasn't allowed, and I'd seen him with his mouth full and a big salami in his hand before. And Marion seemed to have gauged the risk; she smiled at me and said thanks and ate the cake.

'Got a bit of a thing about her, Lofty, have you?'

'No, rubbish! I'm just asking, that's all.' It was after eleven and we were stacking large cartons of juice packs on the juice shelf. Bruno leaned against the forklift and said, 'She's married. He's a bastard though. Met him a couple of times, at work parties and the Christmas do. He used to be a nice guy, I heard, but he's been a right bastard since he lost his job. There's your chance, Lofty.'

'Hey, leave it out,' I pushed two cartons onto the shelf. 'I just think she's nice, that's all.'

'Oh yeah, she's nice all right, Marion is.' He nodded. We carried on working in silence until twelve, then I had to go over to Processed Foods; there was only one woman there, Irina Palmer, and the twenty-kilo flour sacks were too heavy for her. Irina was very nice and she showed me around the processed food aisles once we were done. She smelled quite strongly of cold smoke and she coughed quite a lot, and while I was lifting the flour sacks off the pallet and lugging them to the shelves she'd disappeared in the direction of the toilets.

'Right,' she said and led me along the pasta aisle, 'it's all a question of practice, you'll see for yourself after a while. It's important if a customer asks you.' She coughed and stroked the lapels of her overall. She was about the same age as Bruno and just about as stocky too, and I'd seen them heading for the toilets together a few times; Bruno liked a quick smoke now and then, but not as often as Irina, and he didn't cough like she did either.

'Right, here's the normal spaghetti, then comes chitarra, that's kind of straight pasta, we only have one brand though and hardly anyone ever asks for it.' She was moving quite quickly to and fro in front of the shelf, touching the packets and cartons with both hands. 'Here's the fusilli, they're like spirals, penne lisce, penne rigate, tortellini, tortelloni, macaroni, macaroncini, pappardelle, wide fettucine, then here's the trenette, the same only thinner, rotelle for soups, orecchiette, they look like little ears, and if someone asks for vermicelli they want spaghetti and they're from Sicily.' She pronounced the names of the pasta like a real Italian, moving faster and faster in front of the shelf and showing me all kinds of pasta varieties that I'd never eaten and never even heard of. And then, when she showed me the 'farfalle' and the 'rigatoni', she suddenly said in the same tone of voice, with the same roll of the R: 'You like Marion from Confectionery, don't you?'

I couldn't help laughing. 'All I did was get her a coffee.' And when she nodded and rocked her head like an Italian mama and opened her mouth to reply, I said, 'Yeah, she's really nice.'

'Listen, Christian,' she took a step closer to me, and because she hadn't called me 'Lofty' like most of the others – funnily enough they'd often called me that on the building site as well, even though there were a few guys there even taller than me – well, anyway I knew right away there was something important coming now. 'Listen, Marion's very fragile, I know she doesn't look like it, I mean, she's, how can I put it, she's never at a loss for words, but you mustn't hurt her, do you get me . . . ?'

'No,' I said, not laughing any more. 'I don't want to.'

She nodded and said, 'It's none of my business, but I like young Marion a lot.'

Then the boss's voice came over the loudspeakers, telling us we could clock off now; actually he was only the boss when the other bosses weren't there. I walked over to the staff exit with Irina Palmer, coughing even as she held her cigarettes in her hand ready for the next one, and then we went to get changed.

A couple of weeks passed until I next saw Marion from Confectionery. She'd been working days for a while, but when I didn't meet her in the aisles or at the vending machine after that Bruno told me she was off sick. 'Anything serious?' I asked.

'Don't know,' he said, but I could tell that wasn't true.

'Come on, tell me.'

'Forget it,' he said. 'If you like her, don't ask.'

And then we stacked six-packs of alcohol-free beer on the shelves.

Twenty minutes before the end of our shift – we were

on our last round of the beverages aisles – he said to me, 'Come on, I want to show you something.'

I followed him. We heard Irina coughing in the pasta aisle but Bruno carried on until we came to the fish and shellfish and then he stopped.

We called this section 'The Sea'. There was a large sales counter behind a roller door. Next to it and behind it and all around it were tanks and small pools of live fish, live crabs and prawns, and crates filled with ice and cooled with the dead fish and shellfish in them. The roller door was already halfway down and we ducked underneath it. Inside, the lights were dimmed, only a few strip lights glowing yellow on the ceiling. He took me over to a large tank with a couple of tubes running in and out of it. 'The water has exactly the same salt content as the ocean they come from,' he said. 'Just a tiny bit more or less and they'd die sooner or later.'

They were large crabs, lobsters or something, lying next to each other and on top of each other in the tank, packed so tightly they could hardly move. I went closer up and saw that their pincers were held together with rubber bands.

'They stay in here,' said Bruno, 'until somebody buys them.'

'But their pincers,' I said, and I saw a particularly large crab moving its arms with the tied-up pincers and touching the glass.

'So they don't hurt each other, you see, and so they don't hurt anyone who wants to take them out.'

I squatted down in front of the tank, my face directly in front of the glass. They had strange long eyes, dark telescopic eyes that came out of their little heads like tiny fingers. The lobsters moved around in the water that flowed in and out again through the tubes, but they didn't have much space and some of them looked as if they were dead already or just about to die, lying still between the others. Their long, thin eyes; I don't know why, but their eyes really did my head in. 'Jesus,' I said, standing up again.

'Yeah,' said Bruno. We stood in silence by the tank for a good while then, looking at the water bubbling and the big pile of lobsters.

'Look at that one,' I said. 'The one right at the back, the big bugger. He's got one arm loose.'

'Where?' asked Bruno, and I went round the glass tank and showed him the lobster, which kept opening and closing the one pincer it had managed to get free from the rubber band, opening and closing. It wasn't moving anything else, as if only its one arm was still alive. 'If he's clever . . .' I said.

'You mean he could cut the others . . .'

'Imagine it though,' I said. 'They'd have their work cut out tomorrow morning . . .'

Bruno laughed, then he shook his head. 'I told you, Lofty, they'd just hurt each other.'

We heard the boss's voice over the tannoy – the end of our shift. We ducked out again under the half-closed roller door, Bruno took the forklift to the recharging station, then we went to the staff exit and the changing room. 'Shall I give you a lift?'

'OK,' I said, 'if you don't mind the detour.' I usually took the last bus but Bruno gave me a lift home now and then, even though he actually had to go in the other direction. We hung up our overalls in our lockers, put away a couple of other things, had a bit of a chat with the others, most of them looking tired, we swiped our cards through the machine, and then we walked past the boss, who shook everyone's hand goodbye, down to the staff car park.

'About Marion,' he said in the car.

'No,' I said. 'You don't have to tell me.'

'She has it pretty tough sometimes,' he said, but I just nodded and looked out into the night.

We were standing outside my house. We'd already said goodbye and as he started to get back in the car I said, 'How about a beer – you've got a quarter of an hour, haven't you?'

'Yeah,' he smiled, locking his car and coming back over to me. 'My wife's asleep anyway.' We went inside and sat down in my little kitchen. I took two beers out of the fridge and opened them. 'Lugging beer around all night,' he said and clinked his bottle against mine, 'makes you thirsty, doesn't it?'

'I get hungry as well sometimes with all that lovely stuff we carry around at work.'

'You were pretty daring, that thing with the cake. That impressed her, that did.'

'How do you know that then?'

'It does her good, Lofty, someone treating her nice like that.'

The kitchen window was open slightly and I heard a train crossing the bridge. 'Help yourself to an ashtray if you want to smoke.'

'I will, thanks,' he said. I went over to the fridge and put the ashtray on the table, and he lit up. 'When you get home from work, can you go to sleep right away?'

'No,' I said, 'not usually.'

'Me neither. I've got this bench, out the front, and that's where I sit then, even if it's cold out. I have a wee drink there and I can look at the fields. I like looking at the fields. It's never quite dark, all the lights from the city, you know?'

'Have you got kids?'

'No, we haven't.'

'Sorry. It's none of my business.'

'It's OK.' We fell silent, drinking and both looking out of the slightly open window into the night. He stubbed out his cigarette in the ashtray and drank up his beer. 'I'd better go.'

'I'll see you to the door.'

We said goodbye out the front. 'We could do this again, eh?'

'Yeah, let's,' I said. 'That'd be good.'

He nodded and walked to his car. 'See you tomorrow, Lofty.'

'See you.'

He was very quiet the next day and the days after; we worked in silence and he disappeared straight away after our shift, and I took the bus home. I was usually the only passenger; the bus drivers knew me by now and said hello or 'Home time at last, eh?' And if I wasn't tired already I got tired on the way, leaning my head against the window, and sometimes I even fell asleep but the drivers woke me; they knew where I had to get off. Then at home I perked up again and spent a long time sitting on my own in the kitchen, drinking beer and looking out into the night and waiting to get tired again.

'So you're doing OK are you, rookie?' She stood in front of me, hands planted on her hips, and gave me an angry stare, two small creases above her nose. Her hair seemed to be even shorter now, and her face had somehow got slightly less angular, but perhaps it only seemed that way to me; I hadn't seen her for three weeks.

'How long do I have to work here until I stop being a rookie?'

'If you help me for a minute I'll think about it.'

'Marion . . .' I said.

'So are you coming or not? I asked Bruno but he's busy.'

'I've got things to do as well, but . . .'

'I can ask someone else.'

She turned away and went to leave, but I was standing behind her and said, 'Don't run away, Marion, I'm coming, this crap can wait. I'll always help you if you want, you know that.'

'Rookie,' she said, turning to face me. She pressed her lips together, so firmly that her mouth was a thin line. 'Marion,' I said. 'You talk too much,' she said. 'There's work waiting for us. Well, come on then.' She looked around but the aisle was empty, then she took my hand and set off. She held my hand quite tightly pressed, and I felt her warmth, remembered the warmth on the seat of her forklift, then she suddenly let go and I walked along next to her.

'Bruno says you're doing well.'

'Oh, does he?'

'If he says so it must be true. Irina was singing your praises too.' I wanted to turn off into the confectionery aisle but she took my hand again for a brief moment and pulled me further along. 'I'm standing in on Delicatessen and Frozen Food today.' We went through the open roller door to the cold storage room. I saw her looking over at the vending machine. But when she saw me looking at her she turned her head aside. 'We've got to go to Siberia,' she said. 'We'd better wrap up warm.' She went to one of the lockers and came back with two thick padded jackets and two hats. I helped her into her jacket, then put one on myself. She handed me one of the hats and I put it on her head carefully, pulling it over her short hair. 'Hey,' she said, and I tugged the hat down over her ears. 'I need to see, you know. I've got a list, we have to get loads of stuff for the freezers.' She tugged at her hat, then pointed at a couple of trolleys. 'You go and get two trolleys, or better three, we've got quite a lot to fill up outside.' We put gloves on too, and once we were wrapped up as warm as Eskimos we couldn't help laughing.

And then we were in Siberia, twenty degrees below freezing, our breath came in clouds, and we took large hunks of frozen pork and beef and threw them in the trolleys; it sounded as if we were throwing stones.

'Imagine if they locked us in here, by accident I mean.' I was standing on the little ladder, handing down a large venison loin to her. I could feel the cold even through my gloves.

'You wish.'

185

'Hey, now you're the cheeky one.' I climbed down from the ladder, folded it closed and leant it against the wall. 'Hmm,' she said, 'I guess we'd have to lug meat around all night to keep ourselves from freezing.'

'I guess we would.' We pushed the three trolleys over to another spot. We'd already filled two of them. Our faces were red, our skin felt really tight, as if it were about to tear. 'Brass monkeys in here,' I said.

'Don't be so soft, we're nearly finished.' We were standing close together, the tiny clouds of steam mingling between our faces, and as we were piling crates of frozen pizza in the trolley she suddenly turned to me and looked at me, her hat down to her eyebrows. I didn't say anything, just looked at her. It seemed as if I could feel her breath through the thick padded jacket. 'Nice,' she said, 'it's nice of you to help me.' We stood there like that for a while in silence, then I said, 'Do you know how Eskimos say hello?' And I was surprised how quiet my voice sounded in the big cold storage room, as if the cold was swallowing it up. She looked at me, and I bent my head down to her and rubbed my nose against hers. She stayed still and quiet, not moving, and after a few seconds I felt her nose moving too.

At some point we turned back to the shelves. 'Now I know,' she said. Then we put the last of the pizza cartons in the trolley.

When I got to work the next day I went straight to the beverages aisles. Bruno always came a bit earlier to fetch the forklift from the recharging station, but I couldn't find either him or the forklift.

There were more customers in the aisles than usual for the time of day. Perhaps there were a couple of good special offers on, and sometimes there are just days when people want to go shopping; I've never understood why that is. And I walked along the aisles; perhaps Bruno had something to do in another section, lending a hand, but actually they always gave me that kind of job, and then I saw the boss of 'Shelf-filling/Night'. He was leaning against the whisky shelf, the customers passing right by him, but he seemed not to notice them at all as he stared at the tiled floor. I went up to him.

'Hi boss,' I said, 'I'm looking for Bruno.'

He looked up and stared at me in surprise. 'Bruno?'

'Yes,' I said. 'I'm on Beverages today, aren't I?'

'You'll have plenty to do on Beverages for a while – Bruno's not coming back.' He gazed past me and I suddenly knew Bruno was dead. I felt like I had to vomit, and I leant against the shelf next to the boss. 'He just went and hanged himself. That stupid bastard went and hanged himself.' I felt a fist in my stomach; it wouldn't let me go.

'No one knows anything. I've known him for more than ten years. No one knows anything. Get your forklift and take care of the beverages.'

'OK, Dieter,' I said. I had trouble walking straight, and I kept thinking, 'Bruno's dead. Bruno's hanged himself.'

I met all sorts of workmates as I wandered down the aisles and then realised I had to go to the recharging station. They seemed to know already and we just nodded at each other, some of them looking at me as if they wanted to talk about it with me, but I kept walking until I was at his forklift.

I pulled the big charging cable out of the socket. I'd forgotten to switch the power off first; that was pretty dangerous, all it took was a touch of the contacts. I held onto the forklift and gave a quiet laugh: 'One down's enough for now!' I got in, put the key in the ignition, and then I drove back to the aisles.

There was that smell, of animals and stables. His smell was still in the little cab, and I wouldn't have been surprised if the seat had still been warm. I drove the forklift to Beverages and worked with his smell in my nostrils all night long.

And that smell again, country air, it was fertilising time. I stood on the narrow road leading to the graveyard – I could see it ahead, a little gate, the roof of the chapel – then I turned around and walked back down the road. The funeral would be starting any minute; there were a few workmates there and the bosses, and I'd brought flowers especially, but I walked back through the little village a couple of bus stops outside of town.

I stopped outside his house. It wasn't far from the bus stop; he'd described it to me a few times. It was a perfectly normal two-storey detached house, like you'd find in lots of villages, not one of those old half-timbered ones or anything. The road was empty and I climbed over the fence. Maybe the gate wasn't even locked, that's probably normal in the kind of villages where everybody knows everybody, but I kind of felt inhibited about going into his place through the gate. I walked around the house. A stable, a couple of sheds, chickens pecking away at the ground, further back I saw two cows in a fenced-in field. At first I wanted to go in the stable, but then I saw the bench. It was against the back wall of one of the sheds. I went over to it. I sat down and looked out at the fields. There was a tractor with a trailer in one of them. It seemed not to be moving, and I could only tell by the couple of trees at the edge of the field that someone was driving it. A couple of birds flapped up around it. Why should I go into the stable? I didn't know which beam it was anyway. I watched the tractor.

'Raise the fork right to the top,' said Marion.

'Why?'

'Hey come on, just do it. Bruno showed me it. I don't know, I like it.' I raised the empty fork as high as it would go. The forklift made its usual sounds, a humming and a metallic pling, then I let go of the lever. I tipped my head back and looked up at the fork, still swaying slightly. 'And now?'

'Let it down again, but really slowly. And then keep quiet.'

I moved the lever a tiny bit, and the carriage with the fork lowered itself down again slowly. 'And now? I don't understand.'

'You have to be quiet. Really quiet. That sound, can you hear it, it's like the sea.'

And she was right; I heard it now too and I was surprised I'd never noticed it before. The fork lowered with a hissing and whooshing sound from the air expelled from the hydraulics, and it really did sound like the wash of waves in the sea. The fork came lower; I sat in the forklift, my head slightly inclined. She stood right next to me, one hand on the control panel. 'Can you hear it?' she whispered, and I nodded. Then we listened in silence.

A SHIP WILL COME

She stands up and walks across the room. From one wall to the other. She raises both fists, looking at the white wraps on her hands. A man signed them, that was . . . minutes, hours ago? She stops at the wall and throws a couple of left jabs. She keeps her right hand up at her chin and punches left, left, left again. 'Jab,' says the old man, 'keep those jabs coming, don't show her your right hand too soon.' She watches her shadow on the wall, she bobs and weaves and moves her torso, jabs left, left, and then a punch with the right, left-right, left-right, and then a right without the jab, 'Don't show her your right hand too soon,' she twists her body into the punch, puts her weight behind it and exhales loudly. She pulls both fists up in front of her face and takes a careful look over her shoulder. The room is empty. She holds her fists in front of her face and dances back from the wall and wonders where the old man is. Sent him out myself, she thinks, that was . . . minutes, hours ago? She sent him out,

191

sent her brother out too and the trainer, 'I wanna be alone.'

Still got time, she thinks and goes over to the bench, sits down and leans against the wall. She shifts, feeling the rough concrete through her shirt.

She raises both fists and looks at the white wraps on her hands. The old man put them on for her, holding her arm really carefully, as if her hand were injured. 'Too tight?' he asks. 'No, no,' she says, moving her fingers. Two men are standing next to the old man, watching every move, and she looks up at them for a moment and then at her hands and the old man's hands; they're trembling a tiny bit, or is that her hands? But then they're still again, and one of the men signs on the white crepe. 'OK,' says the other man, looking down at her and raising the corners of his mouth as if he were smiling, and she stares him in the eye until he looks away and turns towards the door. She feels the old man's hand on the back of her neck and watches the men as they leave the room. You go to her, she thinks, and tell her . . . tell her I'm weak, tell her there's no way I can beat her.

Her brother is standing by the door and closes it behind the men. 'Don't show her your right hand too soon,' the old man whispers directly by her ear, and she nods and she's perfectly calm.

She gets up and begins to run across the empty room again. She stops in front of the big mirror. The glass is flecked with streaks and dots, sweat and water, and in the middle there's a large crack. She smiles; before her second professional fight she threw a right straight at the mirror, and then, twenty or thirty minutes later, her right fist broke the nose of the girl standing slightly fearful before her – why don't you move? why don't you dodge? – she could feel it through her glove, and the fearful girl went down on the floor, crouching down more than falling, and let the referee count her out as the blood seeped over her lips. When was that, a year and a half ago, two years ago? She sees herself smiling in the mirror, she moves her torso to and fro, and when her face touches the crack in the mirror her smile is gone.

She stands in front of the mirror, makes a curtsey and smiles and sticks out her chest; her brother doesn't like that. 'You're thirteen,' he says, 'the boys'll come soon enough,' but her brother can't see her now, turning and smiling in front of the mirror and pushing first her left leg and then her right leg forward.

Her brother is somewhere in the big hall, boxing. He took her along the first time, 'So you get out and meet people, Alina,' no, he said 'Alinchen,' she doesn't like that, it means something like 'little Alina' in German, he told her. 'Alinchen,' he said and danced in front of her, throwing straight rights and lefts at the air. They walked there, all the way from the harbour to the training hall, past the big containers and the dockers, the cranes and the ships, then past the market where their father sometimes sends them to buy fish; the fishmongers shout and yell, she's never seen so many fat women and she presses herself close to her brother as he holds her hand tight. Downtown, between all the people and the shops he doesn't dance any more, only throwing straights and hooks again in the side streets and alleyways, teasing her: 'Alinchen, little sister, you're much too small still.'

No, she thinks in front of the mirror as she moves her hips like a belly dancer and sticks out her chest, I'm not all that small. She dances in front of the big mirror and doesn't even hear the voices from the hall, the shouts, the trampling of feet and the smack of gloves on punching bags and sparring partners, she closes her eyes and she's all alone. The woman who used to live in the room next to her and her brother showed her what real belly dancing looks like, but she's not there any more. She had a cassette recorder, and some evenings they could hear music from her room, strange laments but not sad, not too loud because of the rules, and if they had their window open they closed it because the sea outside roared and the gulls and the ships made all their noise. Sometimes she went over with her brother, very quietly because their father, who lived next door with another man they called 'Uncle Toni' even though he wasn't their real uncle, their father didn't want them to go out in the evenings. The door is just pushed to and they open it cautiously. The woman is standing in the middle of the room, in the dark, dancing. Alina can make out the slight curve of her belly, moving in circles to the rhythm of the music, the woman holding up her hands next to her face, now she lifts them higher and places her palms together. They stand in the doorway and watch the woman, who doesn't seem to see them; now her belly is a little round ball, then it disappears in the shadows, and now all they can see is her hips, and Alina puts her hands on her belly and wishes it were so lovely and round and not so flat and thin, she feels her hip bones and wishes she could dance and be one with the music like the woman moving there in the dark. The spotlight of a passing ship falls through the window onto the dancing woman's face, and Alina sees that it's twisted, as if she were very sad and about to cry, but she's silent and dancing. Then the ship's light disappears, it's dark again in the room, the floor begins to sway, here come the waves from that other ship, it must have been a big ship, and their ship pitches and tosses, glasses clink somewhere in the room, and her brother holds onto the door frame, and she holds onto her brother, but the woman doesn't seem to notice anything and dances . . . quietly, thinks Alina.

She throws a right and feels the world champion's nose breaking. Alina knows her name but she doesn't say it, doesn't think it . . . she throws another right, she sees the crack in the middle of the mirror, the floor's going to sway, she thinks, *I'm* going to make it sway, and you're going to fall. Alina moves her torso loosely from her hips.

'Hey kid, you're doing that right.' She opens her eyes and turns around. An old man in a sweat suit is standing behind her, white hair and pretty fat. She feels herself blushing and folds her arms in front of her chest. 'But we only dance in the ring here, kid.' He smiles and beckons her over. 'You here with your brother, are you?' She takes a couple of steps in his direction and nods. 'But if you want to come along you've got to join in, kid.' She shakes her head and wants to go back to their room on the ship. She hears all the noise of the gulls and the ships when she opens the window. 'Can't just stand by the mirror and watch,' the old man says, clenching his fist in front of his chest. 'You're a good mover, no need to be scared . . . no need. Come on, let me show you a couple of things.' He waves a hand over at the punching bags, men standing by them and hitting them, some of them dancing with their feet and moving their torsos. 'But my shoes . . .' She points at her feet. She's wearing suede boots, almost up to her knees, her brother gave her them, he and some of the other boys from the ship went to the warehouses one night, and when he came back he said: 'You're getting a treat tomorrow, little sister.'

Their father told him off, 'Where did those shoes come from, they're much too expensive,' but her brother gave him a shiny black leather jacket and said, 'That's for you, father, we bought them cheap from the Arabs.' Their father turned away and looked out to sea over the rail; he doesn't much like Arabs, but he likes the shiny black leather jacket and wears it every day.

'My shoes,' she says, but the old man shrugs.

'Take your jacket off, roll your sleeves up and come with me.' He turns around and walks over to the punching bags. She stays where she is for a moment, looks in the mirror, tries to smile and sticks out her chest, then she follows him.

'Little sister,' calls her brother from somewhere in the hall, 'Alinchen, you want to box? You're much too small still, and your shoes . . .'

She looks at her feet and takes a left and then a right straight behind it, right on the nose, and she pulls up her guard. 'Damn,' shouts the old man, 'watch out, go back.' And she goes back, goes back to the ropes and touches her glove briefly to her nose, not broken, she thinks and waits and draws her opponent over to her on the ropes and hits out. The right hook she took was good, she only notices that now, she's slightly dizzy, the floor seems to be swaying, but she hits out, left, left, left, two straights, a hook, head, body, head, 'Right,' shouts the old man, 'show her your right,' and then the girl's sitting on the floor of the ring in front of her and looking up at her, eyes wide. The referee pushes her away and she goes into the neutral corner and looks at her shoes as she walks; she has a tiny stone with a hole in it on the lace of her left shoe, her father gave it to her. 'From back home,' he said, 'from the mountains, it'll bring you luck.' She looks at the audience, the hall is pretty empty still, a long way to go before the main fight, she can make out a couple of friends of her brother's fairly far back, boys from the asylum seekers' ship, she raises her fist, they jump up and wave at her and call out: 'Alina, Alina,' and she hears the referee counting. '. . . three, four, five . . .' Stay down, girl, she thinks, the floor sways, stay down.

'So, kid, you OK?' She turns around, the old man's behind her, she didn't hear him coming in. 'Want to be alone a bit? You're starting soon.'

'No,' she says, 'yes,' and sees the old man putting his hand on the back of her neck in the mirror, then she feels it and she's perfectly calm. 'This is your night,' says the old man, 'this is gonna be your night,' and she sees herself nodding.

'Time for you to warm up,' says the old man, and he takes her arms and pulls her boxing gloves on carefully, 'time for us to warm up.'

He takes her right hand, in its red glove now, and lifts it. 'Remember . . .' he says. 'Yes,' she says, 'I'll only show her it when she's open.' She punches her fists together, and he nods and pulls the two big black punch mitts over his hands. 'Hit her over her left hand, just punch across it when she's open.' He takes a couple of steps back to the middle of the little room, holding both hands up with the mitts on them. 'Left,' he shouts in a hoarse voice, 'keep her away from you, don't let the bitch near you!' She punches a left jab, jacking her left leg slightly, breathing out, 'uh, uh, uh,' punching her left hand over and over against her old trainer's big black mitts, him moving now in the middle of the room as if he were a young boxer, 'Hook,' the young boxer shouts and dances from left to right, and she slams left hooks into his mitt, and when his right hand smacks out at her face she just blocks it and counters with her left fist, it's her left over and over, until the old man calls 'And now your right, show her your hard right,' and she punches her right hand into his right mitt, right across his left hand just in that moment twitching to-wards her face, she twists her body into the punch, puts her weight behind it and screams.

She screams, Alina screams, and her brother screams too, 'Alinchen, come to me, quick,' she wants to push the front door closed again but one of the men has his foot in the door. The floor sways, even though they're not on the ship any more, even though there are no gulls and no machines and cranes making all their noise outside in the harbour, even though no lights of passing ships shine in though the window any more and no passing ships take the daylight away, the floor sways, and she holds onto the door frame as the men just walk into the flat. 'You've got to go,' one of the men says, 'you've got to go back.' A couple of the men are wearing uniforms, and Alina knows what that means: back. There was an old Kurd on the ship, one storey above them, and he used to say, 'If they come to take me back I'll go to the captain.'

'There is no captain here,' she said and laughed, but he said he was fast, he said he'd worked on a boat before and he'd cast off, 'And if the helmsman doesn't play along I'll beat him to a pulp.'

'I'll beat you to a pulp!' screams Alina. 'Left,' calls the old man, 'head, body, head! And when she's open . . .' She sees her brother sitting behind her on the sofa and hugging their father, their father looking tiny and disappearing into the cushions, her brother's head on his chest. She pulls her fists up in front of her face, pushing her left leg a little forward and locking her knee as she slams her left fist into the first man's chest. Two or three times she throws a straight left, and the man stops still and looks at her in amazement. 'Right,' calls the old man, 'show her your beautiful right!' she twists her body into the punch, puts her weight behind it and screams.

They walk along the long narrow corridor. The old man is next to her, his arm around her shoulders. She hears the music she asked for in the hall, a song from the mountains; her father is sitting right at the front somewhere, waiting. She looks at the floor and sees the tiny stone with the hole in it on her shoe. Her brother's walking next to her. She punches her gloves together and says, 'Yeah, yeah.' She's pulled the hood of her robe down low over her face. She sees the end of the corridor ahead. She takes a couple more steps and stops a moment. She sees the hall, she sees all the people, she can hear them. The roar of the sea.

YOUR HAIR IS
BEAUTIFUL

He'd been looking for a Lithuanian all around town. He'd met a whole lot of Russians and he'd asked them about Lithuanians.

Kak dyela? How are you? Do you speak Lithuanian? *Nyet?* Do you know anyone who speaks Lithuanian?

He'd bought a whole lot of men vodka on his search for a Lithuanian, and he'd drunk a whole lot of vodka himself.

When he got the tab he made sure they didn't see all the money he had on him. He'd taken everything out over the past five days – all their savings, seven thousand eight hundred marks – and sometimes he imagined his wife laying the bank statements out on the table in front of her and resting her head on her arms (a little place for the weekends, that's what she'd always wanted), but the image didn't touch anything in him. He wandered the streets of the town by the sea, and he felt as if he'd always been there.

He'd met Ukrainians, Poles, White Russians. Out by the canal leading to the small port was a snack van. That was where they usually stood around drinking beer and vodka, and when he came in the morning it was tea and coffee.

Kak dyela? Khorosho. Yeah, yeah. A Lithuanian? Zids is Lithuanian. Zids isn't here right now.

So he waited for Zids at the snack van by the canal leading to the port. He drank beer and vodka, looking at the run-down yachts and ships moored on the banks of the canal. It was getting dark but Zids didn't show up.

The men spoke Russian; he could only understand the odd word now and then. Two Poles were standing to one side speaking Polish. He didn't understand that at all; the only word he knew was *kurwa:* fuck.

Zids didn't show up and he walked slowly along the canal into town. It was nearly dark now, even though it wasn't even five yet. He was cold and he thought for a moment he'd go back and drink another vodka, but then he saw all the lights of the Chinese restaurant and behind it the town steeple. Next to the church was the hotel he'd stayed in when he arrived in town days ago, but now he was staying somewhere else – his training course had been at the hotel; that was the only reason he'd come. He'd only gone along on the first day, listened to the presentations: market expansion, new scanners, customer service, optimising sales . . . He'd thrown the slip of paper confirming his attendance for the first day in the canal the first night but it hadn't fallen in the water, landing on the deck of one of the run-down ships.

The ships. He'd looked at the ships for a long time. Now they were gradually disappearing in the darkness as he walked away from the canal over to the church. He did a detour around the hotel, even though the training course had long since finished and his workmates had all gone home again. The morning after the first night he'd been with her, he'd packed his suitcase and disappeared. A couple of his workmates had called after him as he walked past the breakfast room, but he'd carried on walking out of the revolving door. What had happened to him – was it just her? He hadn't fallen in love, he was sure of that much; or at least he thought so. All of a sudden he didn't know if he'd ever been in love. All he knew was that he couldn't go back home anymore, that he'd stay here in the town where she was. He felt the money in the inside pockets of his jacket – how much had he spent so far? – but he didn't want to think about that, about what came next; it seemed to him as if he could stay here forever.

He took out a stick of chewing gum, unwrapped it and flicked the wrapper away, and put it in his mouth. He didn't want her to smell the vodka. He'd stopped smoking four days ago because she didn't smoke. He'd offered her a cigarette from the nice leather case his wife had given him last year, back when he'd been made deputy manager of the Processed Foods section, although actually only deputy to the deputy.

He couldn't help thinking of his wife as he opened the cigarette case carefully and held it out to her. She was standing in front of him, handing him the case with a smile and saying: For you, darling, for your promotion. It was all still there in his head: his wife, his flat, his job; but the longer he stayed in this town where *she* was, the stranger and further away it all seemed to him.

Cigarette? She'd shaken her head and said first *Nyet* and then *Nein* and then *Danke*. He'd lit one up for himself but then put it out again, washed his hands and rinsed his mouth with the mouthwash next to the sink in the bathroom. He'd looked in the mirror and imagined how he'd put his face up to her hair, in a few minutes, and he'd waited and looked in the mirror until he thought he couldn't stand it any more.

He waited for the traffic light to turn green and then crossed the road. There was a bar on the corner; he'd asked about a Lithuanian in there as well. He heard snatches of words again as he passed the door; it sounded like there was Russian among them again, but this time he kept on walking. He'd go back to the snack van by the canal leading to the port early next morning. Then he'd wait there for Zids, wait as long as it took until he showed up.

He saw the railway bridge at the end of the street; her house was a little way before it. He walked slowly down the dark road. The town was small and he'd been walking all day. A couple of people walked past him; he shoved his hands into his coat pockets. He touched the leather case holding his cigarettes. He took it out and dropped it on the ground. Someone was bound to find it, the next morning when it got light and people went to work. He walked towards the bridge, looking at the dark houses on either side. Only a few of the windows were lit up. The little port was on the other side of town. I bet most people live over that side, he thought; they want to see the sea when they look out of the window.

The house was forty or fifty yards ahead. He looked up at her window; it was dark too but she always had the blinds closed, even during the day; he knew that. He stopped still. What if Zids smoked? He'd offered cigarettes to the Russians he'd asked about a Lithuanian. A nice leather cigarette case like that made a good impression. He went back but he couldn't remember where he'd dropped the case. He squatted down and looked along the pavement. All he saw was a pair of shoes, belonging to a man coming towards him. He got up quickly, walking towards the house, almost running. He was at the door, pressing the bell. Once, twice. He heard the man's footsteps coming closer; he rang again. Once, twice. He heard the footsteps right behind him, the buzz of the door-opener, he pushed the door open, just a tiny gap, squeezed into the corridor, pushed the door shut again and leant his back against it. He waited and listened.

It was quiet outside. Had the man carried on walking? But then he'd have heard him. Or maybe the man had walked past the door at just the moment when he'd pushed it closed behind him, and that had drowned out the sound. He listened to the darkness of the corridor, standing like that for a few seconds, and then she opened her front door on the fourth floor. He tried to make out her footsteps; they were very quiet because she wore slippers, and she'd be standing by the door when he got up there. How often had he been with her now? Six or seven times? He wasn't counting; he wanted it to seem perfectly normal when he went to see her. He felt along the wall, wanting to switch the light on, but then he left his hand on the brickwork and didn't move – now he heard her, thought he could hear her, the quiet tapping of her little feet. He switched on the light and walked slowly past the letterboxes on the wall and up the stairs.

She was standing in the door, one arm against the doorframe. She was wearing a pale blue bathrobe, open at the front, and he saw the red bra and the red panties she'd been wearing on the first day too. He said: Hello, it's me again, and she nodded and smiled. She did smile, didn't she? She took a step aside and he walked in past her. She smelt faintly of sweat. He stopped in the little hallway and said: How are you, *kak dyela*? and she said, fine, and he heard her closing the door and then locking it. Once, twice. He took off his coat and she took it off him, and he tried to lean on her for a moment while she was behind him, but she walked past him to the coat hooks. And you? she asked. Fine, he said and turned around to her and looked at her tiny slippers. Shower? she asked, and he said yes, and started taking off his shirt. Now she was behind him again and pulled the shirt over his head, and he said thank you and raised both his arms. She took his shirt and went into the living room. He watched her through the doorway. There was a television on, the sound down. There was a calendar on the wall above the television, from the new year already. 1995. A couple of horses, green landscapes.

Long today? she asked.

How long, he said.

She laughed. Yes.

Four hours, he said. Four hours again. She put his shirt on the arm of the chair. He took off his shoes and went in the bathroom in stockinged feet. He watched the door as he showered. He took a long shower but she didn't come in. He'd have liked to shower with her, back on the first day even, but he hadn't asked her. He dried himself and looked in the mirror, like the other days. He saw himself taking some of the mouthwash next to the sink and rinsing his mouth out. He put his trousers and his vest over his arm, went out to his coat in the hall and took a couple of notes out of one of the inside pockets; he trusted her.

In the living room was just her bathrobe over the chair; he laid his trousers next to it and went through to her.

The bedroom was small and dark, only one lamp lighting it up on a table with a CD player on it. A couple of CDs lay silvery on the table, without their covers. The blinds were down, a black vibrator on the windowsill.

She lay on her front, her hands next to her face. He sat down next to her on the bed and she turned her head a little.

Four hours, he said, sliding the money next to her hand. She turned on her back and made a little fan out of the notes. Too much, she said, and he nodded and smiled at her and put his hand on her dark hair and said: For you. *Tibya.*

She moved her head and his hand slipped onto her forehead. Baiba, he said, and she folded the notes together and got up and went over to the living room. He took off his socks. They were slightly damp from the bathroom, and he put them on the floor next to the bed. Baiba came back in. She went over to the CD player. She always listened to electronic music, techno or something, no vocals. He hoped she really was called Baiba. On the first day he'd called her Sissi, like it said in the newspaper. Sissi from Lithuania, brand new, young!

207

You're beautiful, Sissi, he'd said, but he didn't know how much she understood.

One hour, hundred fifty. Only with condom.

Yes. *Krasnaya,* he said. He hadn't spoken Russian since school. Do all Lithuanians speak Russian, or only a little bit? He took off his watch and put it down on the window-sill next to the black vibrator. He had to find Zids, Zids from Lithuania. Baiba, he said, and then she lay next to him.

You are really called Baiba, aren't you? he asked and she nodded. He put his finger on the tip of her nose and said her name again. He stroked her bra, and she reached behind her back with both hands and unfastened it. He stroked across the scar between her breasts, like a small triangle. The first time she'd taken off her bra he'd just sat there for a long time, looking at the scar. He leant forwards and touched the scar with his lips. Maybe she had an operation as a child, he thought, a heart defect or something like that, maybe she's twenty now or twenty-two or a bit younger. He kissed her breasts, then he lay on top of her. He pressed himself against her and felt her breathing. 'No,' she said and moved beneath him, perhaps she couldn't breathe properly, and he let her go and laid his head very lightly between her breasts. He had to find Zids. He stroked her legs cautiously, he slipped his hand under her panties, then he had one finger inside her, he pulled it out again, moved his hand beneath the fabric and over her skin and the slim strip of her hair and pushed his little finger inside her and felt her warmth on his little finger. He didn't move it, there was just his little finger inside her and the music and her quiet breathing. He'd never felt his little finger inside a woman, he couldn't remember it, didn't want to remember anything. Everything's fine, Baiba, I'm here. But she kept her eyes closed and he took off her panties. He held them in his hand for a while, then he put them on the windowsill, next to the black vibrator and his watch. Three hours and forty minutes. She opened her eyes and sat up. They were both on their knees now, facing each other. Her hair fell over her face, and he leant his forehead against hers. Your hair, he said, it's so beautiful, but he could see she didn't understand him. She leant forward and pulled his pants down. Zids, he had to find Zids.

He looked at the ceiling. The room was dark but the light from the street lamps fell on the wall next to the window in thin strips.

Baiba, he said quietly, but he wasn't asleep any more and she was gone. There were two more beds not far off from him, and in them were men; he could hear them breathing in their sleep. He'd been sleeping in cheap builders' accommodation for a few days now; almost everyone living here was Polish. He hadn't found Zids; he'd been with her or lying in bed. What if his wife had reported him missing to the police? But disappearing wasn't a crime. Now he hardly thought of the town where he'd lived all those years. He looked at all the lights on the wall. Your hair's so beautiful. He said it very quietly – he'd say it very quietly in her language when he lay next to her again. But he had to find Zids, he'd look for him again, and he didn't have much money left. Sissi from Lithuania, brand new, young!

The man was there; he'd seen him from a long way off. He was a good way ahead of him and he knew straight away that he wanted to go to her. He broke into a run but it was too late; but he kept running anyway, running down the dark road, his mouth wide open. He stood outside the door to her building, the light still burning inside and then going out. He held his hand on the doorknob, pressing so hard that his fingers went white. He raised his hand very slowly, then put it on the bell. He waited, then pressed the bell. Once, twice. Then he pressed the bell all the way in and left his finger on it, one, two minutes. Sometimes she'd got up and turned off the bell. The ringing. Sometimes he'd been lying on her and not moving and heard the ringing. One, two minutes. No, nobody would ring for that long. But the ringing was still in his head, and he wished she'd moan loudly or call his name. Sometimes the telephone had rung too, over in the living room. He stood outside the door and shoved both hands in his coat pockets. He called her, from a phone box, just before he went to her. All she ever said was yes, and then he hung up and left. He stood outside the door, both hands in his coat pockets. Five minutes, ten minutes. Then he went to the railway bridge a few yards along. He leant against the wall under the bridge, watching the door. Then he looked up at her window, but he knew she always had the blinds down. He wished he had his cigarette case now. A train crossed the bridge and he ducked, drawing up his shoulders. The rumbling of the train was above him for a while – it must be quite a long train – then it got quieter and then it was gone. A couple of people walked past him. They walked faster when they saw him but he took no notice of them, only looking at the door across the way. Another train came and he started getting cold, his teeth chattering. He wanted to look at his watch but it was gone. One hundred fifty. Only with condom. The light went on in the corridor. Just afterwards a man came out of the door. The man buttoned up his jacket as he walked down the road. You bastard, he thought, you bloody bastard.

He stepped out from under the bridge, seeing his shadow on the pavement. He pulled his hands out of his coat pockets and then he ran. His footsteps echoed in the road but the man didn't turn around. And when he was right behind him and the man wanted to turn around – he must have heard his footsteps now – he shoved him in the back with both hands, pushing so hard that the man fell. He stumbled over him, holding himself up by the wall, and the man doubled over, clutching his hands in front of his face. What are you doing, please, what . . . ?

You filthy bastard. She was waiting for me, you filthy bastard. He kicked out at him, but then he saw it wasn't the man who'd gone into the house before. He was much smaller, lying there on the ground, and his jacket was completely different. The man before hadn't been wearing a yellow jacket.

Please . . . please . . .

He reached for the man's jacket, feeling the wallet in the inside pocket, then he let him go and ran down the road, over to the other side of the little town, where the canal led to the port.

•

So you're looking for Zids, said the man sitting opposite.

Yes, he said. He'd been with her again, only a few hours ago.

You've found him.

Good, he said. She'd smelled of sweat again, only very faintly, but he smelt it clearly and it didn't go away when he laid his face against her hair and breathed into it.

What do you want from Zids? asked Zids. He had almost no accent.

I've been looking for you for a long time.

Zids laughed. I've been busy. What do you want?

You speak Lithuanian, don't you?

Yes, said Zids, sometimes.

You're Lithuanian, aren't you?

Yes, said Zids. What do you want?

If you speak Lithuanian . . .

Yes, I do, said Zids.

You are Lithuanian?

Yes.

I want you to translate something for me.

Why? asked Zids.

Just because.

Zids laughed and leant back. Just because.

It's very important, he said. He'd taken her bathrobe and undressed her. Come with me. He'd taken her hands and pulled her towards the bathroom. No. She stood before him naked, shaking her head. Three showers today, she said, stroking her hair and her skin. He took the small bundle of money and put a couple of notes on the chest in the hallway, then he opened the bathroom door and said: Come.

Very important,' said Zids, drinking a slug of his beer. How important?

He took the couple of notes he had left and put one of them down on the table in front of Zids.

Hey, hey, hey! Zids picked up the note, folded it up and pushed it back at him. What do you take me for? Money? For nothing? Let's play a bit of dice for your money, then I'll translate whatever you want.

Just a few sentences. Please, he said. He'd stood under the shower and held her tight, stroking her black hair over and over. She trembled although the water was so hot it was steaming. Everything's fine, Baiba, he said, I'm here.

Just one little game, said Zids, putting the dice shaker on the table. Then he picked it up and shook it next to his head like a bartender, and the dice rattled and shook. The two men standing by the counter came over to them.

Tavo gražūs plaukai, he whispered. He was lying in the dirt by the tracks. The man was punching him and he pressed his face into the ballast. No, no one was punching anyone. He was alone. He turned his head cautiously. He could hear trains nearby. *Tu esi geras žmogus,* he whispered. He didn't know what that meant any more. Your hair is beautiful or you're a good person. The piece of paper was gone. In her flat. *Linkiu sėkmės,* he whispered.

He laughed – he knew what that meant. Good luck. Something hurt inside him when he laughed. She didn't want his piece of paper, she didn't want his words – the words he'd got from Zids in her language. It was raining. It was cold and steam came out of his mouth. Now the drops turned white, melting on his coat and his face. The man slapped him in the face. No money, eh? Don't want to leave? She stood by the calendar on the wall, gathering her bathrobe up over her breasts. Baiba, he said, and the man raised his hand but didn't hit him. If she doesn't want a shower, she doesn't want a shower, he said. Was he Lithuanian like Zids? No, she'd said something to the man in Russian when he'd come into the flat. She'd spoken Russian when she was holding the receiver too. He'd been sitting on the couch, the piece of paper in his hand. Your hair is beautiful. She'd pointed at him when the man stood in the doorway. Baiba, he said, but she walked up to the man, pressed herself tight up against him, put an arm around him and spoke Russian, in a very fast, high voice, and pointed at him and the piece of paper he was still holding in his hand. *Tavo gražūs* . . .

How long had he been in this town now? Two weeks or longer? He thought of his wife and his workmates and the training course and the cash and carry. He felt like laughing but he was scared it would hurt again, somewhere inside him.

It's cruel, he thought, dragging a person through the night like that. He was the deputy manager, actually the deputy of the deputy. Processed Foods section. Now he did laugh, and something dribbled over his chin. He heard the trains and felt his coat getting wet. She stood by the calendar and he looked over at her. 1995. A couple of horses.

CARRIAGE 29

I feel myself gradually waking up. I open my eyes. I'm in a train compartment. The train's moving and I look over at the window but all I can see is the reflection of the compartment in the glass. I'm alone and it's night outside.

I get up and pull down the blind. I don't know what I'm doing on this train, I don't know where I'm going, I don't know where I'm coming from, I can't remember any station. I'm a wine sales rep, I know that much, travelling from town to town for years now. I've been to France and Spain as well, but not by train. A white van, full of bottles and catalogues. I sit down again, trying to remember where the van is, where I am. Something's happened but I can't get hold of it. 'A wonderful pinot noir,' I say, 'dry but very fruity, what ripeness, let it roll across your palate, feel it rolling, grown on the best slopes, you can drink it with anything, always, I'll give you three hundred bottles of this wonderfully fruity pinot noir, a truly aristocratic wine, Prince Löwenstein vineyard, three hundred bottles for . . . or let's say five hundred bottles, the good old prince gets better and better with age, you've got a flourishing business going, *noblesse oblige*, as they say . . .' I grab hold of the holdall on the seat next to me; a couple of bottles clink together and I open the bag. Five litre-bottles of cheap red wine with screw caps, one of them almost empty, and I take it out and put it on the little table under the window. It's pretty nasty plonk, I've never sold anything like that, and I shudder as I drink it, and the full bottles next to me in the bag clink again because the train's moving with a judder now, and I rummage in the holdall, finding a vest, nothing else in there, and shove it between the bottles. Was it that clinking that scared me? I try to understand why; I'm a wine rep and a few clinking bottles shouldn't scare me, but as I drink the cheap wine I get the feeling there must have been a monstrous, much louder clinking somewhere and sometime, it can't be long ago, and I drink until the bottle's empty. I screw the cap back on and start to put it in the bag, but then I put it back on the table. No, I've never sold such cheap plonk. I've got plenty of mid-range wines on offer, but good Rieslings as well . . . 'Freimuth Spätlese 2002 vintage from the slopes of the Bischofsberg in Rüdesheim, in the beautiful Rheingau region near Wiesbaden. A wonderful *Qualitätswein mit Prädikat*, pressed and bottled by Alexander Freimuth himself. Do you know what we call the beautiful Rheingau? Teutonic Tuscany. I'll give you two hundred bottles from the best vineyard in the German Tuscany for a special price of . . .' I see images of towns, hotels, restaurants and corner bars, then vineyards I rep for, and the vines growing on either side like waves; I'm sitting in my white van and driving from town to town, wine samples and catalogues, and no trains and no stations.

I pace up and down between the door and the window. It's a smoking compartment but I don't smoke, I gave it up years ago; it's bad for your sense of taste and smell. I search my jacket pockets and find an open orange pack of cigarettes, Ernte 23 brand. Automatically, I take one out, a box of matches in another pocket, and then I smoke and pace to and fro. 'Prinz von Hessen 2004 vintage; Domdechant Werner 2005 vintage; Diefenhardt 2002 vintage from Martinsthal; F for Flick, vini et vita, from the vineyard by the mill.' The names of the wines are in my head, coming out of my mouth along with the smoke from the cigarette I'm smoking even though I don't smoke any more. I grab at the blind and make it snap back up and look into the night through the reflection of the compartment and my own reflection. What's behind the wine? What happened yesterday, what happened today? Why am I going wherever I'm going? I sit down again. I pull the ashtray out of the armrest and put out the cigarette. I don't like the fact that I'm smoking. I'm a wine rep and my sense of taste and smell are among the most important things. That and talking. I take a new bottle out of the holdall. 'Don't be fooled by the screw cap. The fashion's moving away from corks, certainly for mid-range wines. And I'll tell it to you straight, this is a mid-range wine. And to be perfectly honest, it's even lower mid-range. But it's solid, a good solid table wine, a simple French wine but the best you'll get for the price. Simple but good. A good wine for a good bar. And a good profit margin for an honest business, for you, for me and for your customers.'

She must have been standing there for a good while but I only notice her now, even though my eyes aren't closed. 'Your ticket, please.' I hold the bottle between my knees with both hands and put it down on the floor in front of me. I see the ticket collector looking at the empty bottle on the table. If I'm on a train I must have a ticket, so I search my pockets again – jacket, trousers, shirt. 'This train will divide in Nuremberg; you'll have to find a seat at the front of the train then, from carriage 29 on.'

Nuremberg. I've been there before, on business sometime. 'How long before we get to Nuremberg?' I ask. 'About fifty minutes,' she says. She's holding some kind of device, presumably for my ticket, which I'm still looking for. Coins, pens, tissues. She has reddish hair, a couple of strands falling across her face, and I don't know why but I can't help staring at those red strands of hair in her face, and she doesn't like me looking at her like that while I'm still searching through my pockets. She turns aside and now the device for my ticket is right in front of my face. Those red strands of hair – what is it with that red? I try to remember women I've known with red hair but there's nothing, it's something else, this red (the wine? No, not the wine), but I can't get hold of it. I feel some paper in a small inside pocket, folded, and I give it to her. She unfolds it, looks at it for a while, then she takes the device and stamps my ticket. 'There's a twenty-minute stay in Nuremberg, you'll have enough time . . .' She hands me my ticket. 'Yes,' I say. 'Thanks,' and then she leaves, pulling the compartment door to behind her.

I'm holding the ticket in my hand but I'm looking at the wine bottle on the floor in front of me. I crumple the ticket in my fist, then I spread it out on my knee, stroking it smooth again without looking at it, hearing the rustle of the paper and picking up the bottle and drinking a swig. Why would a veteran wine rep like me ever drink this plonk? 'Munich – Bitterfeld.'

I read it over and over again, 'Munich – Bitterfeld, second class, eighty-four euro,' and I ask myself why on earth I'm going home when I haven't been home for almost fifteen years now. Bitterfeld. Huge factories with flames coming out of their chimneys at times. As a child, I often used to stand outside the huge factories, the air like rotting eggs, and imagine that one day I'd . . . it's all very clear in my head, but what's behind the smoke and the flames? I drink, and then I press my hands to my forehead.

'Mind if I have a smoke in here?' A man's standing in the open door; why don't I hear them opening the door? He's wearing a brown cord jacket, and what I immediately notice is his long, thin neck, and it seems to me like I've seen that neck and this man before sometime and spoken to him – his voice seems familiar too. 'I'm sitting further forward, I booked a seat but you can't smoke there. You don't mind me having a quick . . .'

'No, no, of course not.' I look at him and nod but he doesn't seem to recognise me, and maybe I just saw him at the station in Munich, the station I don't remember at all; it's as if someone or something had teleported me onto this train, maybe the cheap wine's to blame, I'm a wine rep though and I can take my drink, but it's not just the station and the train; there's something wrong but I still can't get hold of it. And again I hear a clinking and again it scares me terribly, but it's not clinking at all, it's screeching; the train slows down and then stops. 'Nuremberg,' I say and reach for my bag. 'No,' says the man, sitting opposite me now and smoking. 'It's a while yet to Nuremberg.'

I look out of the window but there's no station to be seen outside, only darkness, and somewhere pretty far off a few isolated lights.

'How far are you going, if you don't mind me asking?'

'Bitterfeld,' I say and wait for him to tell me where he's going, but he just nods and that looks very strange, with his long, thin neck.

'Bitterfeld. Where exactly is Bitterfeld?'

'Near Leipzig,' I say, and he holds out an orange pack of cigarettes to me; he smokes Ernte 23 as well, and I take one out. He gives me a light. 'You'll have to change then, won't you? We're not stopping in Bitterfeld, are we?'

'I don't know,' I say. 'Probably not.'

'You'll want to ask the ticket collector then.' He pulls the ashtray out of the armrest and taps the ash in a couple of times. 'I bet you have to change in Leipzig. I've been to Leipzig. Lovely churches they have there.'

'Yes,' I say. 'Lovely churches.' The train moves off with a jerk, the empty bottle on the windowsill tips over but the man with the long, thin neck holds onto it; he was pretty fast, as if he'd seen it coming. We're moving off now.

'Is it a big place? Bitterfeld, I mean.'

'No, not very,' I say.

'And the churches, are there nice churches there?'

'I don't know,' I say, trying to remember, but all I see is the chimneys and the smoke and the flames.

'You don't often visit Father Yahweh then?' He croaks the word 'Yahweh' strangely.

It sounds almost like he's coughing, and I ask, 'Who?'

'Father Yahweh, our Lord. You do know our Lord?'

'A little bit,' I say. 'I've read about him.' And that's true. I'm lying in a small cheap hotel, I'm waiting until I can fall asleep, flicking through the hotel bible. I reach for the bottle and drink, then I pass it to the man with the long, thin neck. He leans his head back and drinks in large, greedy gulps, and I look at his Adam's apple moving up and down very fast. 'Thanks. The Lord gave us wine.' He hands me the bottle, leaning far forwards as if he were bowing to me or his Father Yahweh, and I drink again, not letting him out of my sight. He's lit up another cigarette; he smokes just as greedily as he just drank. 'Did you see the beautiful churches in Munich? You did come from Munich?'

'Yes,' I say, 'Munich. Lots of churches in Munich.' I've been to Munich on business a lot, although I'd have done better business there as a beer salesman, and I search, search in my head for what happened this time in Munich. And there's that clinking again and a smashing as well, but I can't get hold of it yet, can't concentrate on it either because the man's started talking about his Father Yahweh again, telling me it's all thanks to Father Yahweh that he's sitting here now.

'And he sent me to you, to this compartment.'

'Do you think so?' I say, drinking and handing him the bottle.

Very quietly he says, almost whispering, 'Lots of compartments were empty but I came to this one. Father Yahweh leads me, his rod and his staff guide me, although he has reason to be wrathful at me, and he has great wrath at me, and yet he leads me to the laid tables.'

He's starting to scare me, this man. Now he's drinking and I almost forget that I could use someone to guide me too, someone to clear my head, to give me back all my memories, and I say, 'The Lord's angry with you?'

'You have to say his name,' he says, very quietly again. 'Father Yahweh, his name's Father Yahweh, we have to say his name for him to hear us.'

'Father Yahweh's angry with you?' We use the familiar form of address; I don't know when we switched over from *Sie* to *du*, but it's another thing that makes me think I know him already, as if we'd talked to each other before, but for God's sake, I don't know the man, I'd definitely remember if someone had told me such crazed nonsense before, and what else can I call it . . .

'Father Yahweh put a curse on me.'

'Now which is it?' I say, losing patience now. 'He leads you but he puts a curse on you, what kind of . . .'

'Calm down,' he says, smiling and lowering his head in my direction. 'We have to love Father Yahweh and recognise

Him. And I recognised Him too late, spent all those years without His light, and that's what he's punishing me for, and not just me.'

I close my eyes and press my head against the headrest. I hear him talking, talking about God and illumination and punishment, and for a brief moment there's a memory, the man with the long, thin neck standing very close to my white van, there's a woman too, lying down, and something about her reminds me of the ticket collector, I want to reach out and grab hold of it but the picture blurs, the memories aren't clear, and when I open my eyes I see a small Madonna statue right in front of my face. The Virgin Mary's holding a tiny Jesus in her arms, and at first I get a shock, then I feel the train moving and I think that I've never seen anything as ugly as this. China, or probably just cheap plastic or plaster; white, pink and pale blue.

'Isn't she beautiful? Isn't she absolutely beautiful? The way she's holding the Baby Jesus? If you look really carefully you can see him smiling.'

And I look carefully but all I can see is a tiny line that's supposed to be his mouth, and I say, 'Yes, beautiful.'

He puts the figurine carefully in the breast pocket of his jacket, smiling again or still smiling. I see his yellow teeth when he smiles. He's smoking again or still smoking. 'You ought to visit Father Yahweh in the churches of your town.'

I want to tell him about the huge chimneys with the flames coming out of them but suddenly I'm very tired and I drink and all I say is, 'Who knows . . . my town.'

'Father Yahweh,' he starts again, even though I've

passed him the bottle, but suddenly I think of something and I interrupt him and his smile, which I can't stand any longer, and I ask, 'Who, my friend, who has He punished apart from you?'

He puts the bottle down. He looks at me for a long time, and I can't hold his gaze so I lower my head, as if his gaze had hit something right in my eyes, and I look at the floor and hear him whispering very quietly, 'My wife.'

'Dear passengers, we'll shortly be arriving in Nuremberg, where the rear section of the train with carriage numbers . . .'

The bottles in my bag clink together as we walk along the train. Outside I see all the lights of Nuremberg station, but I have to hurry because the man with the long, thin neck is almost running ahead of me; I see his back, the opened bottle of wine held next to his hip. I'm surprised we've reached Nuremberg already; it seemed like we'd only been sitting in the compartment a few minutes, talking and drinking and smoking. 'Come to the front with me, I'm sitting in a large compartment, there was a space free next to me before.' I'm quite glad he didn't say Father Yahweh saved the seat next to him, and I walk along behind him but I know there's something else, something I have to find out about why I feel compelled to follow him. And as I hurry along the train with him the wines are in my head again – it's as if I needed them so I don't come to a stop and maybe so I can jump out of the train, Nuremberg station, despite the ticket to Bitterfeld – I'm scared as I walk along behind him, maybe of the memories, maybe of the pictures he's going to bring me. 'Herrenberg, Künstler, 2003 vintage; Hupfeld, Winkeler Hasensprung, Riesling Kabinett, 2005 vintage; Georg Müller, 2005 vintage, Hattenheimer Schützenhaus; Rüdesheimer Berg Roseneck, Spätlese, 2004 vintage.' Riesling, it's always Riesling, and I think of the good vintages and the not so good ones, of the good vineyards and the not so good ones, and my white van was full of bottles, wine samples and catalogues and lies.

And suddenly we've slowed down to a crawl. Or he's slowed down. He's walking very slowly and he turns around and puts a finger to his lips. 'We'll be there in a minute,' he whispers. 'Most of them are asleep.'

And they are asleep. Only a couple of little lamps are on above the aisle and they're sitting in the dingy light, in bucket seats with the backs leant back, no one moving a muscle, like space travellers frozen in their sleep between the stars, I think.

'Here we are,' he says, and then I'm sitting next to him and we're drinking in silence, in among the silent spacemen, and then we're moving off. And as if he'd just been waiting for us to move again, he whispers, 'I'm to blame. If I'd recognised Father Yahweh in His mercy and goodness He wouldn't have punished me.'

But I don't reply. I want to ask him, 'Who are you? Where do you come from? How did Father Yahweh punish you?' but it's as if I couldn't talk any more, even though I do want to find out our secret, even though I know there's something between us, something I sense but that he doesn't seem to know, or doesn't want to know. And he talks and talks, and because I don't reply he gets louder and louder, never mind that he told me before that we have to be quiet in here. 'He gave me His light by showing me darkness. You must find the right path before a scourge befalls you too, like it did me. You have to reach your hand out to Father Yahweh so that He gives you His light!' He talks all kind of nonsense, and I stare out of the window into the darkness. We must be passing through a forest or something; there's no light to be seen outside, not even a tiny one, nor out of the opposite window either. And I stare into the darkness; what's behind the darkness? And suddenly the man with the long, thin neck calls out loudly, 'Eli, Eli, lama sabachthani!' I turn to him and see his contorted face next to me in the semi-darkness. Movements to be felt in front and behind us, I hear the whispering of voices, the astronauts awakening although we're not yet at our destination, and he calls out again next to me, 'Eli, Eli, lama sabachthani!' and then, as if nothing had happened, he whispers in my ear, 'That means: My God, my God, why have you forsaken me? And that's what I called out, out loud and over and over again, when He took my wife from me, I called it out although I didn't even know Father Yahweh back then, you see.' I want to ask him how he knew the words then, but I don't reply because I'm afraid of his insane explanation. He gives me a zealous nod; it doesn't seem to bother him that someone behind us just called out, 'Shut up will you, you madman, there's people trying to sleep here!' I see that I'm holding an almost full bottle in my hand; I can't remember opening it, and I drink in great gulps, and he whispers on next to me; it's almost as if I'd only imagined his terribly loud '*Eli, Eli, lama sabachthani,*' but he made the astronauts angry too, on their paths between the stars. 'On your paths, on your paths you'll need Father Yahweh. Without Him, death and damnation await you! Death and damnation, do you hear, you have to turn to Him to escape the punishment for your sins.'

'Sins?' I ask, feeling my tongue stick to the roof of my mouth even though I've just taken a drink, and I drink again in great gulps.

'Sins, oh yes, sins!' He's got louder again suddenly, bending over to me, and suddenly I can't bear to be near him any more; I turn aside and twist away, 'Guilt and punishment,' he calls right in my ear; I drop the bottle; it falls on the open bag at my feet with the other bottles in it, there's a clinking and smashing, clinking and smashing, it can't just be the bottles hitting each other, 'sins, oh yes, sins,' and then I see suddenly, pressing my hands to my temples and my ears, suddenly I see through the crashing and splintering that's getting louder and louder, I see the small blue car at the edge of the road, I see my van, the wine running onto the asphalt, red and white mixing to rosé, I see the man with the long, thin neck stumbling out of the car, a woman caught in the windscreen, not wearing her seatbelt I guess, and she's red, all red, her hair, her face, her clothes. 'I didn't mean it,' I call out and throw the bottle away, just a few sips of Schloss Reinhartshausen, Hattenheimer Wisselbrunnen during the drive, I hear the bottle shattering somewhere, 'Are you out of your mind?' and the man with the long, thin neck kneeling in front of the car, it's smashed beyond recognition on a slant in the ditch by the side of the road, and it looks as if he's praying.

'I didn't mean it,' I say over and over and I want to lean over to him and ask him why he's on the same train as me, why he didn't recognise me, but the man's disappeared, only broken glass on the seat and a large crack in the window pane, and I look out into the night, and there are all these people standing around me, 'Just went crazy . . . threw it right at the window . . .'

I'm bleeding, or is it just wine? I want to get up, the broken glass crunching beneath my feet – where's the man? – but someone's holding onto me. I'm a wine rep.

THE OLD MAN BURIES
HIS BEASTS

He fills his pipe. He chooses his favourite pipe with the straight mouthpiece. He fills the bowl slowly with the tobacco, pressing it down with his thumb. Then he sits down by the window and smokes. A hen runs across the yard. He has to catch it but that'll be hard; it can smell the others lying in the shed. No one wanted to take his chickens. The few people still living in the village have enough hens of their own. And the really old ones don't have any animals any more, only cats and dogs. What's he to do with his dog? Call the vet from the next village to put him down? No. He's had that dog for twelve years, for twelve years Kurt's been sitting in his kennel by the gate, keeping an eye out. Kurt can sense something's not right; he won't stop howling and whimpering. The hen races past the window again and he gets up, his pipe between his teeth, and goes to the door.

There's a willow basket on the bench. He picks it up and walks to the shed. He hears the dog howling and collects the hens' bodies and heads in the basket. The sawdust and the sand by the chopping block are dark with blood. His pipe's gone out, and he taps it out against the axe handle and shoves it in his breast pocket. The bowl of the pipe is still warm. His apron's lying in the corner like a clump of black and red. What a crying shame, he thinks; all those lovely chickens. He could have asked around in the neighbouring villages but he didn't want that – they'd only have asked him why he wanted to give his hens away. And they're his animals; he doesn't want them to end up somewhere else. He has to take two trips to lay all the hens in the little pit he's dug in the garden. He looks over at the fields behind the garden; he'd leased them until two years ago. But he's glad enough that he hasn't got the cows any more; what would he have done with the cows? Behind the fields and the meadows he sees the dilapidated halls and barns that once belonged to the agricultural cooperative. He shovels earth onto the chickens, a few white feathers left next to the pit, and then he goes back to the house.

The hen's still running around the yard. It's slowed down now but the old man's tired and he doesn't want to catch it. He walks over to the kennel. Kurt's disappeared inside, not howling any more, and the old man knocks on the roof. 'Kurt,' he says, 'my boy, my old boy.' The dog pokes his head out and the old man strokes his grey muzzle. He doesn't want to look at him and he strokes him and looks out at the road and the houses, most of them empty. 'Kurt,' he says, 'it's going to be a long day for the two of us.' It's only midday and the sky's blue and the sun's shining after a whole week of rain, and the old man asks himself if he ought to wait until it gets dark, or go for a walk with Kurt in the evening sun. It's not far to the woods, but perhaps it's better to stay by the house. He thinks of the sea, which isn't far either, twenty minutes in the car – but what does he want with the sea? He never used to go to the sea often; that was for holidaymakers. They just used to go for a meal in the old harbour tavern in town every couple of years. What was it called again – The Dancing Sailor? No, that was somewhere else; wasn't it the Seaman's Heart? He's not sure any more.

And he's still thinking about it as he walks down the road to the village. He stops at the old *Konsum* cooperative shop and looks in the window at the empty room. The shop's been closed for years now, and there's nowhere to shop in the next village any more either. He doesn't like the big supermarket in the middle of the fields just outside town. They used to meet here outside the *Konsum* when they came home from work, from the cooperative or the fields. They used to drink beer and talk, sometimes they drank beer and didn't talk, before they went back to their farms and into their houses. Fred, Wee Henry, Walfried, Jochen Schuster and Jochen Meyer – all long gone now or dead.

He wants to remember their faces and their voices, here outside the shop, but there's nothing, and he starts walking again.

'What was that tavern called again?' he asks, fetching the little tree stump he keeps next to the watering cans and the rakes. 'In town, I mean, on the harbour front. You always used to like it there. Maybe we should have gone more often.

You should have said something.' He carries the tree stump over to her, his back aching slightly, and then he sits down. He takes the pipe out of his breast pocket and then he realises he's left the tobacco at home, but he clamps it between his teeth anyway. The mouthpiece fits exactly into the gap. The other old villagers envied him his good teeth; there's just that double gap at the top left. He looks at the empty gravesite next to her. He wants to say something to her, like he always does, he wants to tell her about the last few days, what he's been up to and who he's met, but the old man just chews on the mouthpiece of his pipe and blinks at the sun. He knows most of the people buried round here, he's been to most of the funerals in the last few years, scattered earth and flowers on coffins and urns, and every time he couldn't help thinking of his wife, who he'd buried more than ten years ago. The *Konsum* was still open back then, and afterwards they stood outside the shop window in their suits and drank beer before they went to the village pub, for the 'funeral meats', as he called it. The tree stump he's sitting on has been exposed to the weather and is riddled with woodworm, but it's soft to sit on, as if there were a cushion on top of it. He sits in the sun for a while, closing his eyes. A dog barks somewhere but it's not Kurt. Kurt only knew his wife for two years; they chose him together when old Schultze's Alsatian bitch had a litter. The old man thinks of how his wife trained the dog – Kurt was the fourth dog she'd trained – he thinks of how she sometimes let him in the house at night, when the winter was cold. She got sick that winter but it wasn't the cold to blame. Kurt howled and whimpered for days when she died. It was quick enough. The thing in her head, that's what she called it, and Kurt howled and whimpered so much that he let him in the house, and he ran around looking for her in the house, and then he went quiet. Once, she'd not been gone long, he took the dog along to the graveyard one night. The small iron gate's always open. Do you think he can smell her, down there under the earth, he thought. He let him off the lead but Kurt just ran aimlessly to and fro between the gravestones while he stood by his wife.

The old man wants to think of something good, of the wedding more than forty years ago, but he can hardly remember it any more; all he can see is him dancing with her – was that in the Seaman's Heart? No, they married here in the village, at the Farmer's Inn. How could he have forgotten that, even for a moment? But he forgets a lot and he knows it'll get worse. They celebrated their thirtieth anniversary at the Seaman's Heart, just him and his wife and no guests, and that's the dance – he knows that now – that he remembers. All on their own between the tables.

He carries the tree stump back to the watering cans and the rakes. It's his tree stump but he's not the only one who uses it. He saw old Schultze sitting on it once; he's so old he's buried two wives here.

He walks along the empty village road. It's Friday and he has his appointment at the Farmer's Inn. Once a month he gets his hair cut. Hardly anyone goes to the Farmer's Inn any more, since the last young people left the village and the old ones have been disappearing one by one, but Gerhild doesn't want to shut the place down; she owns the house and she lives above the pub. 'You're pretty much my only customer,' Gerhild always says. The bar room's cleared out, only the round table with the large 'Regulars' sign in the middle's left now.

'Haircut and a beer as usual?' Gerhild's behind the bar doing something with glasses. She doesn't look up; she knows it's him. His footsteps echo in the empty room and he stops still. 'I'll have a *Korn* with it. And bring me the whole bottle.'

The glasses stop clinking; Gerhild looks at him. 'Something to celebrate, Albrecht?'

'Nice weather today. It's stopped raining.'

She nods. 'You take a seat. I'll bring it over and then I'll get the scissors.'

He goes over to the table, pushing one of the chairs out into the room. He hears her opening a beer bottle; the pumps aren't in use any more. Werner, the landlord, died six years ago – or was it seven? He was fifteen years older than her and she's been on her own ever since. She was fifty-nine back then, the best catch in the village, they'd joked outside the *Konsum*, and they'd thought she'd sell the pub and move to town, but she stayed.

She comes over with the beer and a shot glass. The bottle's in her apron pocket, and she puts everything down on the table behind him.

'How are your lads, Albrecht?'

'They want to come and visit again soon. Maybe in September.'

'They should be ashamed of themselves. If I . . .'

'Don't, Gerhild.'

'Sorry. I'll get my scissors.'

'It's all right. You have a glass of wine with me.' She turns around to him and smiles. 'You want me to cut your ears off or something? No, no, you drink on your own, Albrecht.' She walks across the bar room, his eyes following her. He drinks his schnapps and washes it down with beer.

He's drunk three shots by the time she gets back with the scissors and the towel. She spreads the towel over his shoulders. He looks at the tiny white tips of hair falling on the towel and the floor. He doesn't really need to come every month; he's been coming for eight years and it's only a few millimetres of hair every time. He hears the sound of the scissors, feels her fingers on his head. His wife used to cut his hair, before. When she died he left his hair to grow, for over a year. He'd almost gone to seed, like some of the men he knew from the village or the neighbouring villages, who didn't take care of their farms and themselves once they were on their own, until they went too, not long afterwards. But Schultze and Gerhild and her husband the landlord helped him. It took him nearly two years to get back on his feet, more or less. He'd been so tired back then, as tired as he was again now. 'There we are, you're done. Your hair's not growing any faster either.' She laughs. She shakes the hair off the towel and goes to the counter. The old man watches her go, stroking his shoulders and his chest. A few tiny hairs sparkle on his shirt. He fills the glass again and drinks, washing the schnapps down with the remaining beer. He puts a twenty under the bottle and gets up. 'Are you off already?' She's holding a broom and a dustpan.

'Got things to do,' he says, walking past her. 'Bye then.'

'Come by next week. Old Schultze comes in every Wednesday again now.'

'All right, I might come by then,' he says. He's at the door already, wants to turn around to her again, but all he does is knock on the doorframe before he leaves the pub. He used to come here a lot, even as a child, with his father.

The old man walks over to Schultze's house at the other end of the village, where the woods start. There's a lake in the woods not far from Schultze's house, where they used to go swimming sometimes in the hot summers, Schultze and him and their wives. He was there a few weeks ago, stood on the banks for a long time, listening to the quiet hum of the motorway a good way off. He had his swimming trunks and a towel with him but he didn't go in the water; the lake suddenly seemed dark and eerie, he could make out dead white trees on the opposite side.

The old man walks in through the open gate and around the house. The yard's empty; Schultze hasn't had hens for a long time.

They sit in the front room, next to each other on the big leather sofa, drinking brandy. The old man sees the photos of Schultze's two wives on the sideboard. There's a plate on the table in front of them, half a dried-out cheese roll. 'Another good August on its way,' says Schultze. He talks loudly; his hearing's bad. 'Yes, it looks like it.' They clink glasses and drink. For a few minutes they sit there in silence. 'You haven't been over in a long time, Albrecht.'

The old man nods. 'Had a lot to do. I don't go out that much any more.'

'Me neither,' says Schultze.

When the old man went out to the lake a few weeks ago he saw Schultze from far off, pacing to and fro in his yard, from one fence to the other. When he came back from the lake later on Schultze was still on the move, to and fro, from fence to fence, and he wondered where the man got the strength and the stamina at well over eighty; he'd been so tired even on the way to the lake that he'd have liked to have a lie down under a tree.

'I need your gun, Schultze.' The old man's still looking at the sideboard and the photos, and Schultze lowers his head all the way to his chest, leans forward and fills their glasses again.

'For my dog. He's old and sick.'

'Take him to the vet, he'll do it quietly.'

'I want to do it myself, you know?'

'I know,' says Schultze. They empty their glasses in silence, then Schultze gets up and leaves the room.

The old man walks slowly through the village, back to his house. The sun's lower now but the sky's still pure blue. The old man stops outside a couple of houses, looking in at the empty windows. A cat outside a gate, Müller's old farmyard; is that still the Müllers' cat? Cats can cope on their own. Müller's wife moved to town, sheltered housing; she couldn't get rid of the farm. He turns back round to the cat, sitting in the sun and moving its tail. The old man walks along the outside of the field so he doesn't pass the graveyard again. The cloth bag with Schultze's gun in it bumps against his leg as he walks.

'Will one bullet do you, Albrecht? I haven't got many left.'

'Fill it up, Schultze. I don't want him to suffer.'

Schultze nods and loads the bullets into the long magazine. 'I hope it still works. Haven't used it for ages.' Schultze sometimes used to tell stories about the war, down at the Farmer's Inn. The old man can hardly remember the war, but Schultze's nearly ten years older than him.

He walks around the house. He hears Kurt barking. The gun bumps against his leg and he stops still and holds onto the garden fence for support. He stands like that for a while, waiting for Kurt to stop barking. A bee settles on his shirt, and he brushes it off and goes to the gate.

Dear readers,

With the right book we can all travel far. And yet British publishing is, with illustrious exceptions, often unwilling to risk telling these other stories.

Subscriptions from readers make our books possible. They also help us approach booksellers, because we can demonstrate that our books already have readers and fans. And they give us the security to publish in line with our values, which are collaborative, imaginative and 'shamelessly literary' (Stuart Evers, *Guardian*).

All subscribers to our upcoming titles
- are thanked by name in the books
- receive a numbered, first edition copy of each book (limited to 300 copies for our 2011 titles)
- are warmly invited to contribute to our plans and choice of future books

Subscriptions are:
£20 – 2 books (two books per year)
£35 – 4 books (four books per year)

To find out more about subscribing, and rates for outside Europe, please visit: http://www.andotherstories.org/subscribe/

Thank you!

To find out about upcoming events and reading groups (our foreign-language reading groups help us choose books to publish, for example) you can
- join the mailing list at: www.andotherstories.org
- follow us on twitter: @andothertweets
- join us on Facebook: And Other Stories

This book was made possible by our advance subscribers' support – thank you so much!

Our Subscribers

Aca Szabo
Alexandra Cox
Ali Smith
Alisa Holland
Alison Hughes
Amanda Jones
Amanda Hopkinson
Ana Amália Alves da Silva
Ana María Correa
Anca Fronescu
Andrea Reinacher
Andrew Tobler
Andrew Blackman
Angela Kershaw
Anna Milsom
Anne Christie
Anne Withers
Anne Jackson
Barbara Glen
Bárbara Freitas
Briallen Hopper
Bruce Millar
Carlos Tamm
Carol O'Sullivan
Caroline Rigby
Catherine Mansfield
Cecilia Rossi
Charles Boyle
Charlotte Ryland
Christina MacSweeney
Claire Williams
Clare Horackova
Daniel Hahn
Daniel Gallimore
David Wardrop
Debbie Pinfold
Denis Stillewagt
Elena Cordan

Emma Staniland
Eric Dickens
Eva Tobler-Zumstein
Fiona Quinn
Fiona Miles
Gary Debus
Genevra Richardson
Georgia Panteli
Geraldine Brodie
Hannes Heise
Helen Leichauer
Helen Weir
Henriette Heise
Henrike Lähnemann
Iain Robinson
Ian Goldsack
Jennifer Higgins
Jimmy Lo
Jo Luloff
John Clulow
Jonathan Ruppin
Jonathan Evans
Joy Tobler
Judy Garton-Sprenger
Julia Sanches
Juro Janik
K L Ee
Kate Griffin
Kate Pullinger
Kate Wild
Kevin Brockmeier
Krystalli Glyniadakis
Laura Watkinson
Laura McGloughlin
Liz Tunnicliffe
Lorna Bleach
Louise Rogers
Maisie Fitzpatrick

Margaret Jull Costa
Marion Cole
Nichola Smalley
Nick Stevens
Nick Sidwell
Nicola Hearn
Nicola Harper
Olivia Heal
Peter Law
Peter Blackstock
Philip Leichauer
Polly McLean
Rachel McNicholl
Rebecca Whiteley
Rebecca Miles
Rebecca Carter
Rebecca K. Morrison
Réjane Collard
Ros Schwartz
Ruth Martin
Samantha Schnee
Samantha Christie
Samuel Willcocks
Sophie Moreau
   Langlais
Sophie Leighton
Sorcha McDonagh
Steph Morris
Susana Medina
Tamsin Ballard
Tania Hershman
Tim Warren
Tomoko Yokoshima
Verena Weigert
Vivien Kogut Lessa
   de Sa
Will Buck
Xose de Toro

Our first four titles, published in autumn 2011:

Iosi Havilio, *Open Door*
translated from the Spanish by Beth Fowler

Deborah Levy, *Swimming Home*

Clemens Meyer, *All the Lights*
translated from the German by Katy Derbyshire

Juan Pablo Villalobos, *Down the Rabbit Hole*
translated from the Spanish by Rosalind Harvey

Title: *All the Lights*
Author: Clemens Meyer
Translator: Katy Derbyshire
Editors: Bethan Ellis, Ellie Robins, Jamie Searle,
James Tennant
Proofreader: Annie Lee
Typesetter: Charles Boyle
Series and Cover Design: Joseph Harries
Format: 210 x 138 mm
Paper: Munken Premium White 80gsm FSC
Printer: T. J. International Ltd, Padstow, Cornwall

The first 300 copies are individually numbered.